Nobody's Son

MAR 13
CH

Nobody's Son

Zaria Garrison

www.urbanchristianonline.com

Urban Books, LLC
78 East Industry Court
Deer Park, NY 11729

ISBN 13: 978-1-60162-825-1
ISBN 10: 1-60162-825-0

First Printing March 2013
Printed in the United States of America

10 9 8 7 6 5 4 3 2 1

This is a work of fiction. Any references or similarities to actual events, real people, living or dead, or to real locales are intended to give the novel a sense of reality. Any similarity in other names, characters, places, and incidents is entirely coincidental.

Distributed by Kensington Corp.
Submit Wholesale Orders to:
Kensington Publishing Corp.
C/O Penguin Group (USA) Inc.
Attention: Order Processing
405 Murray Hill Parkway
East Rutherford, NJ 07073-2316
Phone: 1-800-526-0275
Fax: 1-800-227-9604

Nobody's Son

by

Zaria Garrison

Dedication

This book is dedicated to my son,
John Devanté Garrison

Acknowledgments

First and foremost, I must thank God who is the head of my life and the true author of all of my books. He is the reason that I write what I write. The reason I am who I am. I give Him all the glory and all of the praise.

Thank you to all of the readers who've read my books in print or e-book. I realize that without readers there would be no writers, and for that I am eternally grateful.

Lastly, thank you to my husband, my son, my friends, and my family for continuing to support me as I live my dream of being a writer.

Prologue

Wayne blinked his eyes trying to focus in the darkness. His abductor had just taken off the blindfold that had been surrounding his face and blocking his vision. It really didn't matter because all he could see in every direction was blackness. Seated on a hard wooden chair his hands were bound behind his back and his feet were tied tightly to the chair legs. After untying the blindfold, his abductor reached for the ropes, but to Wayne's disappointment, he tightened them, making sure that he could barely move.

"Who are you, and what do you want from me?" he screamed into the darkness. His voice echoed, then faded into silence.

His captor had not spoken a word since he'd grabbed him from behind just as he was exiting his condo. Wayne was about to get into his car when he felt a gun poking into his back. Even though he was petrified, he didn't panic. Instead, he calmly cooperated while praying that the assailant would take his wallet and leave, but the abductor didn't want money or Wayne's brand-new slate-blue Cadillac Escalade. He wanted Wayne, and he quickly blindfolded, bound, and gagged him, then threw him into the back of a utility van. They drove around for a while, and Wayne soon began to feel motion sickness. His stomach buckled, and he felt nauseated. Finally, the van stopped, the door opened, and Wayne felt himself being dragged forward with his arms pinned tightly behind his back. He heard a large garage door screech loudly, open, and then close behind him, so he assumed he was in some sort of warehouse building. Wayne was unsure how much time had elapsed since his abduction, but he guessed it had been several hours. His body was sore and fatigued, and he was beginning to get sleepy, so he imagined it was late in the evening. The rumblings in his stomach also let him know that it was way past dinnertime.

"I'm hungry. Aren't you at least going to feed me?" he screamed.

"Later," a gruff voice said.

Chapter One

Two weeks earlier . . .

Semaj sighed as he sat in the waiting area of the bakery. His bride-to-be, Ellen, was glowing with excitement as she waited anxiously for the baker to bring out wedding cake samples. Semaj had no idea when he'd proposed six months earlier that his weekends and some weekdays would become consumed with cake tastings, color palettes, wedding invitations, and all things bridal. He had been bored to tears when Ellen tried to explain to him the difference between emerald, moss, apple, and hunter green while she was choosing bridesmaids dresses. It took all of his strength to stay awake when she droned on and on about the pros and cons of whether to have tulips or roses in her bouquet. Semaj wouldn't know the difference between Chantilly lace and burlap, but Ellen knew, and it mattered greatly when she was choosing her bridal gown. All of the details bored him to tears, but he loved Ellen Winston with all of his heart and thanked God every day for bringing her into his life.

Most people, including Semaj, considered him a loner. He was raised by his grandparents, who both passed away during Semaj's senior year in high school. Their sudden deaths left him alone and on his own. He'd managed to work his way through college with a myriad of different part-time and odd jobs, which eventually led to his career. While attending college, Semaj took a job in the mail room of a local news station. Following graduation, he became an intern, a reporter, and eventually worked his way up to anchor. He was proud to be one of the most respected and highly paid anchors in the city. Although he anchored the nightly news, his passion was the special projects he found himself involved in. He'd dedicated his career to helping people find missing loved ones. He'd assisted people in finding long lost siblings, former lovers, and even parents.

Feeling bored as they waited for the baker, Semaj pulled out his iPhone and began to check his messages. An unfamiliar name in his e-mail inbox caught his eye just as the bakery owner entered the room with a plate full of assorted cakes.

"You guys are going to love these samples," she exclaimed excitedly.

"I hope you don't have anything with strawberries in it," Semaj said. He noticed several pieces of cake that were pink in color sitting on the tray.

"Your fiancée told me that you are allergic to strawberries, but I included a few for her to taste anyway. Many couples choose to have a different flavor of cake for each layer."

"Baby, don't worry, we will be sure that you don't get any of the strawberries today or on the wedding day," Ellen assured him.

Semaj shook his head as he realized that once again he was only along for the ride and that nothing he thought, felt, or wanted would be taken into consideration. Like an obedient fiancé, he took several bites of the chocolate, red velvet, and white chocolate mousse slices of cake, then smiled politely, without offering an opinion. Almost two hours after they arrived at the bakery Ellen had finally made her choices and they were free to go. She rattled on and on in the car like a monkey in a tree about the flavors and style she'd chosen while he politely nodded and pretended to be listening.

After dropping Ellen at her apartment, Semaj drove home, took a long hot shower, then plopped down on his sofa wearing only his boxer shorts. He turned on the television in search of any sports-related programming before finally settling on a high school football game. Pulling out his iPhone, his eyes wandered once again to the unfamiliar e-mail address.

"Those spam blockers ain't worth a crap," he muttered to himself as he debated whether to open the e-mail. Finally, his curiosity got the best of him, and he clicked on it.

Dear Mr. Matthews,

I am contacting you regarding a personal matter that is strictly confidential, but could be of financial benefit to both of us. I have information regarding a family member that you have been searching for. Please contact me at 555-4216 so that we can discuss this further.

Sincerely, Gwen Johnston

At first glance, Semaj believed the e-mail to be one of the many he often received from spammers pretending to have money that was left to him by an unknown relative. In the end, those types of e-mails usually ended with a request for a bank account number to transfer money into a foreign account. Semaj felt a chill down his spine, however, and he knew instinctively that this e-mail was different.

Sometime following Semaj's birth and before his first birthday, his parents split up and he lived alone with his mother in Chicago, Illinois. He had no memory of her at all because shortly afterward, his mother died in a house fire. An anonymous stranger pulled Semaj from the burning structure while his mother perished inside. As a child, Semaj often questioned his grandmother about both of his parents, but she refused to give him any details. Whenever he'd ask, she would scold him about digging up skeletons from the past and admonish him to let sleeping dogs lie. All he knew of his mother was that her name was Allison, and she was only nineteen years old when she died. He knew nothing at all about his father. Once he'd asked his grandfather to at least tell him his name, and the expletive that passed his papa's lips shocked him so much that he never asked again.

Semaj suddenly realized that he'd been staring at the e-mail for several minutes. He glanced at the clock and decided that it was still early enough for him to make the call. He quickly dialed the number and waited.

"Hello?"

"May I speak with Gwen Johnston?" he asked politely.

"Who's calling?" the woman on the other end inquired.

"Semaj Matthews . . . um . . . you . . . um . . . She sent me an e-mail." Nervousness caused him to stumble over his words.

"Mr. Matthews, I am so glad that you called. I'm Gwen, and I think I have some information that you'd be interested in."

"Is this for a news story?" he asked.

"No, this is personal." Gwen cleared her throat. "The word on the street is that you don't know who your biological father is. Well, I do."

Semaj hesitated before responding. He'd heard those words before, and it never seemed to pan out. It was a decision that he'd come to regret, but Semaj had decided against hiring a professional to help him look for his father. Instead, he'd traveled to Chicago and started asking questions of people that he believed knew his mother. As a former reporter, he felt that the real stories came directly from the streets. It was a tactic he used often as a journalist, and it had never failed him, until he began looking for his father.

He'd discovered that one of the problems with talking with people on the street was that for a price they'd make up the story they thought you wanted to hear. One individual had even approached him claiming to be his father and requesting money, but he quickly recanted his story when Semaj asked for a DNA test.

He took a deep breath as he waited to hear Gwen's tale. "You are correct. I have been searching for my natural father. What do you know about him?"

"I'd rather not discuss it over the phone. Can you meet me somewhere?"

Semaj rolled his eyes. "I could, but I won't. Let me be frank with you, Ms. Johnston. I've heard a lot of different stories and outright lies since I began looking for my father. People tell me that they know something, when in truth, they don't know a thing. For that reason, I have become very skeptical and distrustful. No disrespect to you personally, but I'm not coming to a meeting that could turn out to be just another wild goose chase."

Gwen chuckled. "You have his fire and passion, that's for sure."

"A lot of people are passionate. Look, if you don't have any real information to share, then I'm sorry, but I'm going to have to end this call."

"Okay, you were born in Townsend Memorial Hospital in Lawrenceville, North Carolina, on May 28, 1975. You barely weighed five pounds because you were four weeks premature. You were born with a birthmark in the shape of a strawberry on your left hip. Coincidentally, you also are allergic to strawberries. Everyone in your father's family has the same allergy."

Semaj was stunned. The circumstances of his birth were something he rarely discussed. He'd never told anyone that he was born in North Carolina, and his grandmother had not shared the information with him until his sixteenth birthday. At the time, he begged for a copy of his birth certificate and told her it was so that he could obtain his driver's license. Truthfully, he'd hoped it would contain his father's name, but it did not.

"What's my father's name?" he asked, trying to hide the excitement in his voice.

"I don't want to say over the phone. Your father is a very famous man."

Semaj's heart sank as he suddenly began to find Gwen's story suspicious. There was no way that his father could be famous. It had to all be another bad joke. Out of nowhere he felt the Holy Spirit speak to him.

"Go meet her. She's telling the truth," the Spirit said.

"Have you ever been to Vonnie's Soul Food on Peachtree Street? I can meet you there for lunch tomorrow," he said.

Chapter Two

Ellen knocked several times on the door of her sister Jenise's apartment. While she waited for an answer she cautiously looked around the parking lot of the complex. Although she'd grown up in the area, Ellen felt more than a twinge of anxiety whenever she had to return to Sand Poole Manor Apartments. When her parents had moved into the complex in the early eighties, it had been a nice place to raise a family on a modest income. Over the years, drugs and gangs had turned it into a frightening war zone that Ellen detested coming into. However, she loved her sister dearly, and no matter what, she had to make sure she was okay.

"Hey, Auntie Ellen," her niece Aaliyah said, as she opened the front door.

Ellen reached down and gave her niece a hug, then quickly entered the apartment. In her mind she was wondering what alarmed her more, the fact that her five-year-old niece had just opened the door without inquiring who was on the other side, or the fact that the child should be in kindergarten and not at home answering the front door.

"Where's your mommy?" Ellen asked.

Aaliyah took a seat on the floor in front of the television and picked up a bowl of cereal, then pointed down the hallway. "She's been in her room all day," she said. "I think she might be sick, cus she hasn't come out, and I didn't go to school."

"Where's your daddy?"

Aaliyah shrugged her shoulders as she shoveled a spoonful of cereal into her mouth.

Ellen walked down the hallway and lightly tapped on her sister's bedroom door. "Jenise, it's me. Open the door," she said.

A few seconds later her sister peeped out of a crack in the doorway. "Is Aaliyah with you?" she asked.

"No, she's watching cartoons."

Jenise opened the door and backed away, allowing her sister to enter, then quickly closed it again. Ellen gasped loudly as soon as she saw her sister's face covered in bruises. Jenise's lips were busted and swollen, and her left eye was a garish shade of purple.

"I don't want Aaliyah to see me like this. It would frighten her," Ellen said.

"It's frightening to me. Jenise, why do you let him do this to you?" Ellen didn't wait for an answer to her question because she had asked it many times before and the answer was always the same. Instead of listening to Jenise say once again how much she loved her husband, Ellen walked to the bathroom and came back with a cold towel that she pressed lightly against her sister's face.

"He's been under a lot of pressure this week, that's all, Sissy. He apologized, and it's okay. Don't worry about it."

Ellen slowly shook her head. "What kind of pressure could he possibly be under? He doesn't even have a job."

"He's trying to get his music career started. You know that. If he took a full-time job, he wouldn't have time to practice his music or record his CD. You just wait and see; my hubby is going to be the next Kirk Franklin."

"I bet Kirk never punched his wife because he was under pressure."

Jenise scowled at her sister. "I don't know why I even bothered to call you. I mean, you've never liked Reggie anyway."

"I like him just fine. It's what he does to you that I can't stand."

Jenise began to cry. "The only reason I called you is because I need you to take Aaliyah for a few days so she won't see me like this. If you can't do that, you may as well leave."

"Don't cry, Jenise. You know I don't mind taking my niece. She told me that she missed school today, but I'll make sure she goes tomorrow, and then she can spend the weekend with me. She thinks you're sick, so I won't tell her any differently."

"Thank you, Sissy." Jenise wiped her tears and gave her sister a big hug. "Are you sure she won't be in the way? I know you have lots of wedding planning stuff to do. I got fitted for my bridesmaid's dress the other day. It's beautiful."

Ellen knew her sister was trying to change the subject and deflect her attention away from her face, but she didn't protest. "As a matter-of-fact she can help me. I've got a few do-it-yourself projects to complete, and she's pretty good with a glue stick." Ellen smiled for the first time since entering the apartment.

"That's great. Aaliyah loves spending time with you."

Ellen flashed another fake smile. It pained her to see her sister in such a state. Her physical appearance was ghastly, but Ellen also felt pain for what was going on inside her sister. She couldn't believe that Jenise saw nothing wrong with the fact that her husband chose to hit her whenever he was upset, under pressure, or just in a bad mood.

During their seven-year marriage he had sprained
Jenise's arm, fractured her jaw, and placed dozens of
bruises all over her body. Each time he swore that he
was sorry and begged for her forgiveness. Ellen begged
her sister to leave him, but nothing seemed to penetrate that shell of marriage. Ellen wholeheartedly believed in the sanctity of marriage and was excited at the
thought of marrying Semaj, but she couldn't help but
wonder if saying marriage vows sucked the brains out
of some women. She watched her outgoing, boisterous,
happy, single sister turn into a reclusive, quiet, with-
drawn married woman, who used her wedding vows as
a reason to stay with a no-good man.

"God wants me to remain with my husband. God
doesn't approve of divorce," Jenise had often said. Ellen only half agreed because no matter what scriptures
Jenise chose to quote, there was no way she could convince her that God wanted her to be used as a punching
bag.

Ellen left the bedroom and helped Aaliyah pack her
lavender miniature suitcase with her favorite pajamas,
her sneakers, socks, underwear, several pairs of jeans,
and matching blouses. When they were done, they returned to the living room and Ellen asked Aaliyah to
wait for her by the front door.

"I just want to say good-bye to your mommy, and
then I'll be right out," she said.

"Can I say bye to Mommy too?" Aaliyah asked. Her
little face was filled with excitement.

"She's sick, honey, and . . . well . . . I don't want you
to catch what she has."

"What about you, Auntie Ellen? How come you won't
catch what Mommy has?"

Ellen loved Aaliyah's inquisitive nature and detested
having to lie to her. "Tell you what, let's both just say
good-bye through the door," she suggested.

After saying good-bye to her sister, Ellen and Aaliyah went down the steel staircase of the building and out to Ellen's car. Ellen popped the trunk and placed Aaliyah's suitcase inside, then closed it.

"Auntie Ellen, isn't that Uncle Semaj over there?" Aaliyah asked.

Ellen looked in the direction that Aaliyah was pointing and saw her fiancé hugging a strange woman. She stared at them for several dumbfounded moments before finally getting into her car and driving away.

Later that evening, Aaliyah happily ate the dinner of spaghetti with meatballs that Ellen cooked for her. After taking a bath, she begged her auntie to read her a story, but she fell asleep before Ellen finished reading three pages. Ellen laid the book on the nightstand by the bed, and then gently kissed her niece on the forehead. As she left the room, she clicked off the light, while leaving a soft blue night-light burning in the corner near the window.

As soon as she was inside her bedroom she dialed Semaj's cell phone number and anxiously waited for him to answer.

"Hello."

"Hey, it's me," she said softly, while trying to keep her voice from shaking.

"Hi, baby, how was your day?" he asked cheerfully.

"I saw you and that woman over at Sand Poole Manor. Who is she?" she blurted out. Ellen did not mean to say it so abruptly, but after waiting all day to speak to him she was unable to hold it inside any longer.

"What woman? What are you talking about?" Semaj asked.

"I was at Sand Poole Manor today picking up Aaliyah, and we both saw you with a big-boned light-skinned woman. I saw you hug her. Who was she, Semaj?"

"I wasn't at Sand Poole Manor today. You guys are mistaken."

Ellen mentally scratched her head while rewinding the afternoon through her brain. "I was positive that it was you. Besides, Aaliyah pointed you out first."

"I don't know who you saw, but I can assure you that I was nowhere near Sand Poole Manor today. Anyway, I was just in the middle of working on a story for tomorrow's show, and I need to finish it, so I'll call you back later."

Semaj quickly hung up before Ellen could protest.

Chapter Three

Semaj tossed and turned for several hours, unable to rest. In their entire relationship he had never lied to Ellen. In his heart he knew that she was his soul mate, his best friend, and his queen. Every fiber of his being was deeply in love with her, and he was furious with himself for telling her a bold-faced lie. He deeply regretted it, but he just didn't know how to explain to Ellen things that he himself was struggling to believe.

Semaj turned over and looked at the clock. Although it was close to three o'clock in the morning he knew his cousin would still be awake, so he quickly dialed his number.

"Yeah," his cousin Rip said as he answered.

"Hey, man, I need a favor," Semaj said.

"Anything for you, Cuz; what is it?"

"I need you to cover for me with Ellen. She saw me at Sand Poole Manor with a woman today, and well, of course, she's upset. It was all innocent, but I can't explain it to her yet."

Rip suddenly began paying closer attention. "I'm intrigued. Are you sure your visit to Sand Poole was innocent?"

"Yes, I had a meeting with a woman who had some information about my biological father. The whole conversation has me freaked out, and I just can't explain it to Ellen yet."

"So, Gwen finally decided to call you? I'm really glad."

Semaj sat up in his bed. "You know Gwen?"

"Come on now, Cuz. Do you really think there is a woman living in these projects that I don't know?" Rip laughed loudly.

Semaj laughed along with him. "I should have known that big, pretty, yella girl had not gotten past your radar."

"You know me, man. I love the honeys with the big juicy booties, and so do you. So are you sure it was all innocent? I mean, you've never asked me to cover for you with Ellen before."

Semaj's mind went back to his conversation with Gwen. "Yeah, it's innocent. She told me who she believes my natural father is, and honestly, I think she's correct. I mean, I've heard so many outlandish and wild stories over the years, but she had some real facts to share. She knew things about me that nobody could have told her, and she certainly could not have found on Google. She knew where I was born, and that I have a strawberry allergy and birthmark. She knew the name of the building that caught fire when my mother was killed. It was almost scary talking to her, as if she could see right through to my soul. After all these years of searching, I think I've finally found my real father." Semaj grinned with excitement.

"So, are you gonna tell me who it is or keep me in suspense?" Rip asked.

"I . . . I can't. Not yet."

"Are you kidding me?" Rip exclaimed. "We've been tight as long as I can remember, and you know I love you like the brother I never had. I encouraged Gwen to talk to you, and now you don't want to tell me what she said? That's messed up."

Semaj tried his best to explain. "I am going to tell you everything, but not right now. I need time to process the information within my own spirit before I can talk about it. Man, what Gwen told me is so mind-blowing that I'm honestly afraid to say it aloud. That's why I lied to Ellen, and I need you to back me up. Trust me, man, when the time is right, I will tell everyone everything."

Rip sighed loudly and yawned. "All right, man. You know I'm in your corner no matter what, so when you are ready to talk, I'll be ready to listen."

"Thanks for understanding, I really appreciate it."

Semaj hung up the phone and finally drifted off to sleep. He awoke the next morning to the sound of his phone ringing loudly. "Hello," he mumbled sleepily.

"Semaj, where are you? Our appointment with the caterer is at nine this morning, and it's way past eight thirty. Did you forget?" Ellen wailed.

Semaj looked over at his bedside clock. Eight-forty-five stared back at him. "Ellen, sweetheart, I am so sorry. I overslept, and honestly, I did forget. Why didn't you remind me about this appointment last night?" he asked as he jumped out of bed and rushed to the bathroom.

"I was going to remind you, but you never called me back last night. What's going on with you, Semaj?"

"Nothing, baby . . . Nothing's wrong," he stammered. "I was up late working on, um, a missing person's report, and I fell asleep and forgot to call back. I also forgot to set my alarm clock. Just let me hop in the shower and I'll be there to pick you up in twenty minutes."

"No, we'll be late for the appointment. I'll go ahead and drive my car and leave now. Just meet me there as soon as you can."

"That sounds good. Text me the address and I'll be there in a jiffy." Semaj hung up the phone and rushed into the bathroom.

Ellen was about to say, "I love you" when she realized that the line was dead. She quickly texted the address to Semaj, then left her apartment. Ellen arrived at the catering company office just in time to make their appointment. A friendly blond gentleman greeted her at the front desk.

"Hello, Miss Winston, it's so good to see you," he said. "Our personal chef Cedric is excited to meet with you and your fiancé." He looked over her shoulder. "Is he parking the car?"

"Um, no, he's running a little late, but he should be here soon," Ellen replied.

"That's fine. If you'd like, I can escort you into the meeting room, and you can begin looking at menu choices. I'll show your fiancé in as soon as he arrives."

Ellen nodded her head in agreement and followed the gentleman into a small conference room. After she was seated comfortably, he laid out a series of menus in front of her with dozens of choices for her wedding. She and Semaj had decided to have a small wedding ceremony at their church with only a few guests and a medium-sized reception. The guest list was less than 100 people, but she'd insisted that they have one splurge item, and that was the catering company.

Cedric Grier, the owner and head chef, was a former classmate of Ellen's who supplemented his college finances by cooking and serving meals to his fellow students. The first time Ellen bit into his spicy fried shrimp with orange sauce, she told him that when she got married he would be the one cooking the meal. He was flattered and happily agreed. Now, almost ten years later, he was one of the most successful and sought out caters in the city of Atlanta. He'd catered parties for celebrities like Tyler Perry and most of the area's rap artists and sports stars. After becoming engaged, Ellen felt intimidated calling him and asking him to be a part of her small affair, but he happily agreed. He'd also agreed to give her a 25 percent discount, which helped tremendously in her quest to convince Semaj to have him as their caterer. However, even with the discount he was still the most expensive item on their wedding budget.

She'd been flipping through the menus for about fifteen minutes when the door swung open. "Ellen, it's so great to see you again," Cedric exclaimed as he walked into the conference room. "It has been ages, but you are still fine as ever." He pulled her into a big hug.

"Thank you, Cedric. It is great seeing you also." She reached up to hug him back.

"I'm sorry I'm running a little late. I just had a meeting with the producers of *Revelations* and they put in a bid for me to cater their season-ending cast party. My wife loves that show." He sat down in a chair facing Ellen.

"Don't apologize, I wasn't on time myself. Besides, you are big time these days. I'm just proud to know you and glad you are willing to cater my little wedding." She grinned excitedly.

"Oh, please, I'm nothing special. I'm just a country bumpkin from Columbus, Georgia, who loves to cook and eat, as you can tell by my big frame." He patted his ample belly and laughed. "I feel blessed that God is allowing me to be successful doing the thing that I love most. When I broke my ankle and lost my football scholarship freshman year I thought my life was over, but God had other plans. I'm thankful, that's what I am."

Ellen nodded in agreement. "Yes, I agree, you have a lot to be thankful for. I mean, you were one of the best running backs in the state, and everyone believed that you'd play professional football one day. It had to be disappointing to have it all taken away from you so quickly."

"It was all part of God's plan, Ellen. Sometimes in life we chase after our dreams without consulting God, and then we are devastated when those dreams don't materialize. As I was lying in the bed in that hospital with my leg in a cast I couldn't imagine doing anything other than running a football down the field. My entire focus was on getting well and getting back out on that field. Then when my scholarship was revoked, I realized that I couldn't play football if I wasn't still in school, so I had to find a way to pay for my education until I was well enough to play. That's when I began cooking for other people just to make ends meet, and I realized that I loved it more than I loved playing football. I love trying out new recipes and creating new dishes from unique items. It's truly my passion."

Ellen's eyebrows scrunched up in confusion. "I thought that I remembered you eventually playing on the team during our junior and senior years. I didn't realize you quit after that injury."

Cedric laughed heartily. "I rode the bench those two years. My ankle never healed enough for me to play seriously again, but I no longer had the heart for it anyway. I went back to the team and received a partial scholarship, but I knew that football would end with college and that catering would be my life's work."

"Well, I'm certainly glad for that. I've been skimming over these menu selections, and I must admit that I am totally overwhelmed by all of the wonderful choices that you have. It's going to be very difficult to decide." Ellen spread the papers out on the table.

"Where's your fiancé? I bet he could decide quickly. No offense, but brides tend to be picky, but when I speak with the groom they make quick decisions."

Ellen looked at her watch and suddenly wondered why Semaj had not arrived yet. "He should have been here by now," she answered. "Excuse me a moment while I give him a call."

She allowed the phone to ring until voice mail picked up. She hung up without leaving a message and dialed again, and again. Semaj still did not answer. Ellen sat staring at the phone with a bewildered look on her face. "He's not answering his phone. That's not like him at all. I hope nothing is wrong," she said.

"I'm sure there's no need to worry. He's probably stuck in traffic."

Ellen shook her head. "Semaj always answers his phone. He has a Bluetooth for when he's in traffic. My fiancé is a news anchor, and he specializes in locating missing people. He gets lots of tips by phone, so he always answers."

"Semaj Matthews from Channel twenty-seven, is that your fiancé?" Cedric eyes widened with surprise.

"Yes. Are you a fan?"

"Wow, and you called *me* big time? Semaj Matthews helped locate my younger sister who was kidnapped last year. Cyndi Lawson is my baby sister." Cedric noticed the confused look on Ellen's face. "We have different fathers, so we have different last names," he explained. "Your fiancé found her when the police weren't doing anything for us."

"Are you talking about the nine year old who was taken from the playground in her neighborhood over by Sand Poole Manor?"

Cedric nodded rapidly. "Yes, she had been missing for over a week, and the police did not have any leads. They were doing all they could, I suppose, but it just wasn't enough. So we decided to contact Semaj. He found her a few days later and even escorted her to my mom's house. I saw on your paperwork that it was the Winston-Matthews wedding, but I had no idea that Semaj Matthews is your fiancé."

Ellen beamed with pride. "Yes, he's the love of my life. We met at a picnic at our church about two years ago and got engaged last year." Ellen glanced at her watch again. "He's really very dependable and never misses appointments. I'm so sorry he's not here yet."

"Do not apologize. He's probably out helping some other frantic family locate their loved one. It's no problem at all. I don't have any other appointments scheduled for today so we can wait as long as you need to for him to arrive."

Sighing loudly, Ellen looked at her watch once more. "Unfortunately, I can't wait all day. I took the morning off from work, but I am scheduled to be there by eleven. It's almost ten now."

"I'll tell you what I'm going to do. You go ahead and pick out three menus that you like, and then you can go. We'll set another appointment time and for that one I will prepare each of your selections for you and Semaj to taste and make your final choices from."

"That's a good idea. Let me just look over this and see which three choices fit into our budget," Ellen replied.

Cedric covered the price sheet with his massive hand. "Forget the prices. I know I told you that I'd give you a 25 percent discount, but that was before I knew that you were marrying Semaj Matthews. My family owes him a debt of gratitude, and he refused to take any money after bringing my sister home. I will prepare whatever you choose, for no charge. It's the least I can do." He smiled broadly.

"Cedric, you don't have to do that. Semaj is dedicated to his work, and he doesn't do it for money. The way that you feel that cooking is your calling from God, he feels the same way about his work with missing persons. I mean, he enjoys being an anchorman, but finding people and bringing them together with loved

ones, now *that's* his passion. The discount is very generous, and we appreciate it. We don't need any more
than that."

"I will not take no for an answer, Ellen. If you try
to write me a check for payment, I will just tear it up.
My little sister means the world to me and my whole
family. Without Semaj's help, she might not be with us
today. I know he doesn't do it for the money, and no
amount of money in the world could be paid for what
he did for us. Just allow me to pass on a blessing to you,
please."

Ellen slowly nodded her head. "All right, if you insist. Let me call Semaj once more to see if he's close
by and can help me choose." Ellen silently prayed that
Semaj would finally pick up the line. When he did not,
she decided to leave a message. "Hey, sweetie, it's me.
I'm still waiting for you at the caterer's office. Are you
lost? Please call me back." She hung up the phone and
turned to Cedric. "Can you give me a few moments to
make my choices?"

"Of course, take your time. When you are done, just
give your choices to David at the front desk, and he
can also help you schedule your tasting appointment."
Cedric stood up and walked toward the door. "And
stop worrying. I'm sure Semaj is fine. He just got busy
today, that's all. It's not a big deal."

Ellen took her time making the three menu choices,
hoping that Semaj would arrive in the nick of time to
help her out. She also dialed his number several more
times, but there was still no answer. After stalling as
long as she could, she finally took her selections to the
front desk and gave them to David.

"Do you want me to go ahead and schedule your tasting appointment, Miss Winston?" he asked.

"Um, no, not yet. I need to speak with my fiancé so that I can check his schedule."

"That's fine. Just give me a call at least three days in advance so that Cedric has time to prepare. It was a pleasure seeing you today."

Ellen smiled politely and left the office. She checked her watch again once she was inside her car. *It's almost eleven. If I don't leave now I'll be late for work,* she thought.

She slowly pulled her car out into the busy street and turned in the direction of her job. Less than a mile down the street she noticed Semaj's car heading in her direction. *"Great, he's almost two hours late. I don't believe this,"* she thought to herself.

She decided that she'd call him at the next stoplight so that she could alert him that she was already gone. As his car got closer Ellen noticed another person sitting in the passenger seat. He sped past her going in the opposite direction and did not notice Ellen staring at him chatting happily with the same woman she'd seen him with in Sand Pool Manor the day before.

Chapter Four

"Mr. Matthews, I'm sorry that I called on such short notice, but your dad doesn't give me much notice before he comes into town," Gwen said.

"Please, call me Semaj. Mr. Matthews is so formal," Semaj answered.

She giggled. "I'm sorry. Semaj it is then."

The two of them were inside Semaj's car on their way to a meeting with his biological father. As he drove, Semaj tried to calm his nerves at the prospect of actually seeing him face to face.

Earlier that morning, he'd just stepped out of the shower and heard his cell phone ringing. When he answered, an excited Gwen was on the other end. "Mr. Matthews, your dad is in town. If you are up to it, I can take you to see him," she'd said.

"What are you talking about? I know what you told me yesterday, but I haven't had a chance to check your story out. I'm certainly not ready for a family reunion with this guy."

"I thought you said you believed me. What do you mean you need to check my story out? Look, I have no reason to lie to you. I just thought that you wanted to know who your father was and get a chance to meet him."

Semaj tightened the towel around his waist and sat on the edge of his bed. "I do believe you, but I just felt that I needed more proof, that's all. I mean, you have to admit that it's a lot to take in all at once. How long is he in town? Maybe you can take me to meet him next week."

"He's going to be here for about a month, I think, but today is the only day that I can take you to him. His schedule is tight, and this is the only day he's going to be free during his entire visit."

"How can he be too busy for you? I mean, didn't you say that you are his cousin? I'd think he'd make time for his family. He must be one of those celebrities who's gone so Hollywood that he's forgotten where he comes from."

"That's not it at all. The fact is that whenever he's in the area he makes time to see his relatives, who are here, but he's not here on vacation. He's working. I got a call this morning from his publicist, and she told me that he's free today. Look, if you don't want to go, that's fine. I just assumed that this was important to you."

Semaj sat thinking for several seconds. Although he'd told Gwen that he planned to check out her story, the truth was that he didn't need to. He knew in his heart that the story she'd told him was absolutely true, regardless of how totally unbelievable it was. During their meeting the day before, Gwen had told Semaj that she'd found out about him from an older family member who'd since passed away. There had always been rumors in their family that her famous cousin Wayne James had a son "floating around out there somewhere," as they put it. The story had been passed around with whispers within the family for years, but no one had confirmation of it. After hearing the story from her Aunt Sarah Mae, Gwen decided to find out if it was indeed true.

Her original motives had not been noble. She'd hoped to locate the son, and then sell the story to a tabloid newspaper for thousands of dollars. With that in mind, she'd spent hours researching in the library and online until she'd put the pieces of the puzzle together. Her first big clue was a marriage license she'd found proving that her cousin Wayne had married when he was only eighteen years old. Then she did a search for the woman he'd married and discovered that she'd died in a tragic house fire. She'd told Semaj that she realized this was the same fire that he'd been taken out of by an unknown hero. At that point, Gwen was convinced that the stories she'd always heard as a child were definitely true. She then began a search for the baby who'd been listed under the name of Wayne James, Jr. She'd hit one dead end after another when searching for him. She'd even contacted a reporter and tried to sell the story with just the limited information she had, but they were not interested.

Shortly after that, Gwen met Rip at a party in Sand Poole Manor. The two of them hit it off almost immediately. One night while sipping wine in his apartment and chatting, he told her about his cousin Semaj who was looking for his biological father. As he talked, Gwen realized that the story had eerie similarities to the long lost son of her cousin. Her only issue was that the names didn't match. After meeting Semaj, the two of them came to the conclusion that his grandparents had been responsible for changing his name and had given him their last name. For that reason he'd never even known his mother's married name.

"Mr. Matthews, are you still there?" Gwen asked.

"Um, yes, I'm sorry. I was just trying to decide what to do. You've given me such a huge amount of information in such a short time."

"I know that, but I believe that we waste time sitting around thinking about what we are going to do in our lives. Sometimes you've got to just jump in and sink or swim."

"It's just all so fast. If it's the reward you are concerned about, don't be. I know I told you that I needed proof, but I believe you. I'll go ahead and pay you the money."

Gwen grinned. "Well, that's great, but that's not why I'm calling. I honestly would love to be there when you finally meet your father. I understand if you need more time, but it may be months or even years before he's back in town."

"You know what, Gwen? You're right. I have been secretly dreaming of this day as long as I can remember. I mean, I always told people that I didn't care who my father was and that I didn't want to meet him or find him, but it was all a lie. It's been my strongest prayer."

As he drove to Gwen's apartment, Semaj excitedly imagined what it would be like to finally meet his father. For years, he'd watched him on television and admired him as an actor. He could hardly believe that his dad wasn't just any Dad, but he was the man known as "America's Favorite TV Dad." On his TV show, Wayne James was father to three rebellious teenage sons. Each week, he managed to solve their problems with wisdom, love, and faith. Semaj admired the relationship that his character had with his sons. However, Wayne's fatherly wisdom did not come from a staff of writers or end on television. In his personal life, he was also the father of five sons. Semaj had heard him tell a reporter once that he had dreamed of being a father since he was a young boy, and although God had not blessed him with a wife, he'd blessed him to be able to adopt. Over the course of several years, he'd adopted each son individually and often told people that he planned to adopt more. His sons ranged in age from four years to seventeen. Semaj grinned as he dreamed of finally having real siblings.

He'd just pulled up to Gwen's building when he noticed his phone ringing and suddenly remembered his appointment with Ellen. He reached for it to answer, then realized that he did not know how to explain to her what he was about to do. Instead, he opted for allowing the phone to roll over to voice mail; then he turned the ringer completely off.

"Pull around to the back of the hotel," Gwen told him as they pulled into the parking lot. "We can't go in the front entrance. We'll have to take the service elevator up to his room."

Semaj did as she instructed and tried to stop his hands from shaking. His whole world seemed to be moving in slow motion as they stepped off of the elevator and walked the short distance down the hallway. He felt like a little kid as he stood waiting for the door to Room 734 to finally open. Inside, he was screaming, *My daddy's in there. Daddy, Daddy, open the door, Daddy.*

Finally the door opened, but it wasn't his dad looking back at them. Instead, it was a huge man who resembled King Kong. His face, his build, and his whole body mimicked a gorilla. Semaj felt frightened just to be in his presence.

"Hey, Doug," Gwen said, and smiled at him. "We're here to see Wayne."

Semaj watched in awe as King Kong's face spread into a wide grin displaying perfectly white teeth.

"Hey, Gwen, I was hoping you'd come by today. Who's your friend?" Doug asked.

"Um, this is Semaj. I hope Wayne doesn't mind, but I brought him along to meet my famous cousin."

Doug stepped away from the door and opened it wider. "I'm sure it's cool. You guys come on in."

They walked into the beautifully decorated suite, and Semaj looked around. He found it hard to believe that he'd been brought there by a girl who lived in the projects, while her cousin lived such a lavish lifestyle. He found it even harder to believe that this cousin was his dad.

Doug offered them a seat in the living-room area of the suite, then excused himself to go get Wayne. Semaj sat next to Gwen and clasped his hands tightly in his lap. Nervously he bounced his knee up and down.

"Relax, Semaj," Gwen said; then she reached over and held his knee down with her hand.

"Now that I'm here, I'm wondering if this isn't a big mistake. I mean, what am I going to say to him? 'Hi, you don't know me, but I'm your son.' This is crazy."

"What's wrong with that? The truth usually works best," Gwen answered.

"Like I said, it's crazy. I've changed my mind, Gwen, I'm leaving." Semaj stood up to leave just as Wayne walked into the room.

"Gwen, it's good to see you, Cuz." He greeted her with a warm smile and a hug, then he turned in Semaj's direction. "Who's this?"

Turning around, Semaj looked into his eyes while resisting the urge to rush into his arms and hug him tightly. Instead, he extended his hand. "I'm Semaj Matthews." He searched his face to see if the name sparked any indication that he knew who he was.

"Oh, yes, Mr. Matthews, I've seen you on the local news. You have quite an impressive following here in Atlanta. It's a pleasure to meet you." He shook Semaj's hand, then took a seat in a large chair. "Please sit down and make yourself comfortable."

Semaj slowly sat down while staring in Wayne's direction. "It's a pleasure to meet you also," he said.

Wayne smiled, then turned his attention to Gwen. "So, Gwen, how is your mom doing? I hope I get a chance to see her while I'm here visiting," he said.

"She's doing great. She had to work today, or she would have come over with me. I think she plans to come when she gets off this evening." She glanced over at Semaj, who was still staring awkwardly at Wayne. "Besides, I brought Semaj along, and he really needs to speak with you about something important. I thought it would be best if there were not too many people around. It's kind of personal."

"Personal?" Wayne looked over at Semaj "We've never met. What type of personal business could you possibly have with me?"

"Well . . . I . . . um . . . Gwen told me . . . well . . . It's kind of hard to explain," Semaj stammered.

Confused, Wayne looked back and forth between the two of them.

"He's your son," Gwen blurted out.

"He's my *what?* My sons are back in California with their nanny. What's this all about?" Wayne asked.

"Your son. He's your son. The one from your marriage, the one that's been lost for all of these years," Gwen said.

Wayne shook his head. "I've never been married, you know that, Gwen. If this guy told you he's my son, he's a con artist."

Semaj cleared his throat and finally spoke. "My mother's name was Allison Matthews. She died in a house fire when I was a baby, and I was sent to live with my grandparents."

"Is that supposed to mean something to me?" Wayne answered. "I have never been married, and I don't have a son. Now I'm going to ask you both one more time, what is this all about?"

Semaj could tell by the tone of his voice that Wayne was quickly becoming agitated by the whole conversation. "I'm sorry. Gwen told me . . . Well, it's not important what she told me. I apologize. Obviously, we've made a big mistake."

"Gwen told you something?" Wayne bellowed. "What exactly did Gwen say?"

"Never mind," Semaj said, then stood up. "Gwen, let's just go. I told you this was a waste of time."

Wayne stood up as well. "Gwen, are you guys trying to run some kind of scam on me? I know that you are in between jobs right now, but if you needed money, all you had to do was ask. I've always helped you in the past, and I don't mind helping you, but I will not tolerate things like this."

"No, it's not a scam at all," Gwen insisted. "I've heard stories all my life about your long lost son and your first marriage. So I did some research, and I found Semaj and brought him here to meet you. This is not a scam, I swear it."

"I've heard those stories too, but unlike you, I know better than to believe every rumor that I hear at a family picnic," Wayne huffed.

"Aunt Sarah Mae told me everything," Gwen said.

"How dare you bring my late mother into this!" Wayne yelled. "I don't know what you think she told you, but I have never been married. I do not know anyone named Allison Faye Matthews, and this man is not my son."

"But . . ." Gwen began to speak, but was interrupted.

"Gwen!" Semaj yelled unexpectedly. "I said, let's go. This is a colossal waste of time." He turned to face Wayne and looked him straight in the eye. "Mr. James,

I'm sorry we bothered you. I promise it won't happen again."

Without another word he stormed out of the room and rushed down to his car without waiting for Gwen. He started up the engine and was about to drive away when he saw her running through the parking lot after him.

"Semaj, wait!" she yelled.

He turned off the engine and lay his head on the steering wheel while he waited for Gwen to get into the car.

"I'm so sorry about this," she said breathlessly as she climbed into her seat. "I was positive that my research proved that you are his son. Please forgive me. I'm sorry I put you through this."

"Don't apologize. It's not your fault." Semaj slowly raised his head and looked over at her. "Your research was absolutely right."

"I don't understand. If you believe that, then why did you walk out?"

"I looked into his eyes, and I saw something when I said my mother's name. I can't explain what it was, but I'm positive that I saw it. Then he said her whole name. I never mentioned that her middle name was Faye. He knew her, and he was married to her, but he left us. He doesn't want me. He didn't want me then, and he doesn't want me now. That's why he's denying every-thing. Don't you get it, Gwen? He doesn't want me as his son." Semaj lay his head on the steering wheel again and struggled to fight back tears, unwilling to cry in front of Gwen.

"Maybe he just needs time to digest this new infor-mation. I tell you what, why don't we wait a few days, and then I'll call and talk to him about it. He's probably just in shock and didn't know how to react," Gwen said.

Semaj suddenly sat up and wiped the tears that had escaped and fallen onto his face. "No, don't call him. I'm done. I wanted to know who my father is, and now I know. He's nobody to me. Do you hear me, Gwen? He's nobody."

Chapter Five

Jenise dipped a Q-tip into a bottle of peroxide, then dabbed it onto the cut just below her right eye directly on her cheekbone. Looking into her bathroom mirror, she watched silently as it bubbled and cooled the pain in her cheek. All of the other bruises from her most recent altercation with her husband had cleared up and she was hoping that if she was able to heal the cut on her face she could cover it with makeup before Ellen brought Aaliyah home the next day.

"Jenise, what are you doing in there?" her husband Reggie yelled.

"Nothing, I'll be out in a minute," she yelled back.

"Hurry up. I want you to see this. I got ten more followers on YouTube this week."

Jenise stepped out of the bathroom and stared at him. "I thought you got followers on Twitter, not YouTube. What are you talking about?"

Reggie was sitting on their bed with the iPad Jenise had given him for his birthday sitting in his lap. "Dang, girl, do you ever listen when I talk? Yes, I get followers on iPad, but I put up some videos of my music on YouTube, and I have people who follow that also. If the right person sees my work online, it could be my big break."

"Oh," Jenise answered with little enthusiasm. She still had not been able to get rid of the headache he'd given her three days earlier when he'd punched her repeatedly in the face, so she silently hoped he did not want her to listen to any loud music. She lay down beside him on the bed and turned toward the television. "You wanna watch a movie?" she suggested.

"No, I'm busy working on my music, girl."

"Can you keep it down a bit? I have a horrible headache." Jenise slowly rubbed her fingers in circles on her head.

"You always got some kind of ache. If it ain't your head, it's your stomach. Then yesterday you were throwing up." Reggie stopped playing his video and put his iPad down. "Don't tell me you're pregnant again. We can't afford another baby, Jenise," he said angrily.

"I am not pregnant. I just don't feel good. Can you go to the store and get me some Goody headache powders?"

"Yeah, if you got some money, and if you buy me a beer." He held out his hand expectantly.

Jenise struggled to sit up on the bed. Her head was pounding even harder than earlier. She stood up and walked across the room to get her purse. The next thing she knew, Reggie was standing over her looking worried as she lay sprawled out on the floor.

"Jenise, baby, are you okay?" he asked. "You've been out for almost five minutes."

"I guess I got dizzy and fell. Help me up." She held up her hands to reach for him.

"No, I've already called nine-one-one. Just stay put until the paramedics get here."

Jenise reached up and put her hand over the cut on her cheek that had not yet healed. "What if they ask me about this?" she said.

"Just say it happened when you fell, Jenise."

There was a loud, urgent knock at the front door, and Reggie ran to answer it. A few seconds later, he returned with the paramedics following behind him.

One of them was a tall Caucasian man with dark brown hair. He looked down at Jenise on the floor and immediately noticed the bruising on her face. "What happened here, Miss?" he asked.

"I was walking across the room, and I just fell. I've had a headache for about three days," she answered.

The paramedic knelt down beside her. "Have you experienced any vomiting or nausea?" he asked.

"Yesterday I threw up a few times," she answered.

The paramedic looked at Jenise's bruising and touched her face gently. He turned and gave Reggie a disgusted look, then turned back at Jenise. "Have you, um, *fallen* any other times in the past week?" he asked, then looked at Reggie again.

"No, today was the first time." She noticed that both paramedics were now glaring at her husband. "I'm fine, really. I just got a little dizzy. If you'll just help me up I'll be fine." Jenise reached out her hand, but the paramedic was still staring at Reggie. She tapped him on his shoulder to get his attention and extended her hand once again.

Ignoring her hand, the paramedic continued asking Jenise questions. "How did you get that bruise on your face?" he inquired.

"Oh, I bumped into the wall or something."

"Could that something have been your husband's fist?" he asked.

Reggie rushed over to where they were and stood towering over the paramedic. He was only five foot seven, but with the paramedic on his knees, it gave him a false sense of superiority, allowing him to raise his voice. "Look, you can't come in here making crazy accusations like that. I've never put my hands on her. She told you she bumped into the wall." He looked down at Jenise and gave her a look that demanded she back him up.

"He's telling the truth, honestly. I'm okay," she said to the paramedic, then turned to her husband. "Reggie, help me up, honey."

Reggie reached down and assisted Jenise to her feet with exaggerated affection and helped her to the bed. "My wife is fine now. You guys can leave."

The paramedic stood to his feet and looked down at Jenise lying on the bed. He walked past a glaring Reggie and sat next to her. "Miss, you may have a head injury. I suggest you allow us to take you to the ER so that you can receive treatment."

"She's not going anywhere with you," Reggie declared.

Ignoring him, the paramedic continued speaking to Jenise. "It's your choice, Miss. If you want to go we'll take you, but we can't make you go."

"What kind of head injury?" she asked.

"I'm not a doctor, Miss. Based on your symptoms, I think it would be best to have a doctor take a look at you."

Jenise nodded her head, and the paramedic held out his arm for her to take.

"Jenise, are you crazy? This guy just accused me of punching you. Don't you dare leave this house with him."

Reggie was standing on the sidewalk outside their apartment still screaming her name as the ambulance pulled away from the curb.

"Shoot! Now what am I gonna do?" he asked no one in particular.

"You should've gone with her," a voice from behind him said.

Reggie turned around and saw Rip standing a few feet away from him on the sidewalk. "Big Rip, I didn't know you were out here. Oh, well, I guess I can't call you Big Rip anymore since you dropped over a hundred pounds. What's up, man?"

"Nothing's up with me. Why didn't you go to the hospital with your wife?" Rip asked.

"Man, she didn't need to go to the hospital. She got dizzy and fell, that's all. Now we gonna have hospital bills that we can't pay. It's just a waste of time, that's all."

Rip looked at him strangely. "People don't just get dizzy and fall for no reason. It could be serious. You want me to give you a ride over to Piedmont Hospital?"

"Naw, man, thanks, anyway. Jenise's car is here. I'm gonna head on over there myself. I'm just going to change clothes right quick."

A short time later Rip watched Reggie pulled out of the complex in Jenise's car, but instead of heading in the direction of the hospital, he turned and went the opposite way heading out of the city.

He drove for about a half hour before arriving at his mother's house. He was concerned about Jenise, but he was more concerned that the paramedics intended to call the police and report her bruises. It had happened before, and he'd managed to avoid the questions and accusations by leaving the area for a few days. As he hugged his mother hello, he decided that he would call Jenise in a few days to make sure it was okay for him to return home again.

Rip was on his way back to his apartment when his cell phone began ringing loudly in his pocket. He unlocked his door and walked inside and sat down on the couch before answering.

"This is Rip," he said.

"Hey, Rip, this is Ellen. Have you seen Semaj? I've been trying to reach him since yesterday with no luck."

"Nope. I haven't talked to him in a couple of days myself."

"I'm worried sick. He missed an appointment yesterday, and I've left several messages for him, but he hasn't called back. He didn't anchor the news tonight. I called the station, and they said that he called in sick. I went by his apartment, but he's not there."

Rip scratched his head and thought for a moment. "You're right, that is not like Semaj at all. Listen, if you want me to, I'll see if I can find him."

"Could you please, Rip? I was angry at him because I thought I saw him with another woman, but now I'm just worried that something terrible has happened to him."

Rip laughed. "If I don't know anything else I know that my cousin loves you more than a fat kid loves cake. He would never cheat on you. If you saw him with a woman it was probably a contact for a story or something."

"You're probably right, Rip. I'm just so worried that I can't think straight."

"Listen, I'm sure he's fine. Like I said, I'll see if I can find him, and then I'll call you back. Oh, by the way, how is your sister?"

"Jenise is fine, I suppose. I've been babysitting Aaliyah all weekend for her. I'll see her tomorrow when I drop Aaliyah off. I'll be sure to let her know you asked about her."

"No, that's not what I meant. I saw her taken away in an ambulance about an hour ago while I was out taking my walk. That little jerk she married left shortly after that, but I don't think he was going to the hospital. I was just checking to see if she was all right."

"Oh my God, I had no idea. What happened?" Ellen held on to the phone tightly afraid to keep from dropping it in shock.

"I'm sorry, I thought you knew. Reggie said she fell."

"I bet she fell—right after he pushed her," Jenise said. "I'm on my way over there now, Rip. Call my cell phone if you hear anything about Semaj."

"I will, Ellen. You just take care of your sister, and I'll take care of Semaj."

After hanging up the phone with Ellen, Rip immediately called Gwen.

"I took Semaj to meet his dad, and it didn't go well at all," she told Rip. "It's not my place to give you all the details, but all I can say is that he was pretty upset by the whole thing."

"Do you know where he was going after he dropped you off?" Rip asked.

"He didn't say, but I could tell he needed some time alone. Is everything okay, Rip?"

"I'm sure it is. I think I know where to look for him. Thanks for your help, Gwen," Rip said before hanging up the phone.

Two hours later, Rip pulled into the gravel driveway of the home in rural South Carolina that Semaj had shared with his grandparents. Rip was not surprised to see Semaj's car parked haphazardly in the backyard. After his grandparents' deaths, he'd refused to sell the house or even rent it out. Rip had asked him about it once, and he'd told him that he just didn't have the heart to get rid of it. Instead, he'd allowed one of the town's residents to put a house trailer in the back field in exchange for being a caretaker of the house. Semaj paid the utilities, and whenever he needed to get away, he always came to the one place that he considered home.

When Rip walked into the unlocked back door, he found Semaj seated at the kitchen table eating a plate of fried chicken with mashed potatoes and green beans that the caretaker, Miss Minnie, had cooked for him.

"You want some?" Semaj offered. "Miss Minnie made plenty."

"Don't sit there acting like everything is perfectly normal. What's going on with you, Semaj? Ellen is frantic. Why haven't you returned her calls?"

Semaj took a bite of his chicken leg and slowly chewed it before answering. "I can't talk to her right now. I needed some time to myself. Is there anything wrong with that?"

"Yes, there is, when you disappear like a thief in the night after missing an appointment with the woman you are supposed to marry in a few weeks." Rip pulled out a chair and sat down at the table. "Look, Gwen told me that you met your dad and it didn't go well, but you can't hide out here eating chicken and pretending it didn't happen."

"Says who?" Semaj answered, and took another big bite of his food.

Rip sighed, realizing getting through to Semaj was going to be much harder than he had expected. "Just tell me what happened with this guy," he asked.

"I thought Gwen already told you."

"She didn't give me any details. She felt that you should do that. Now, whether you like it or not, I'm here, and I'm waiting for you to talk. Take all the time you need, I'm not going anywhere." Rip got up from the table and went to the refrigerator. "You got any red Kool-Aid?" he asked while peering inside.

"It's on the second shelf," Semaj answered. "If you haven't eaten you can go ahead and fix yourself a plate too."

Rip fixed himself a large plate of chicken and green beans but declined the potatoes. In the past two years he'd dropped 190 pounds, and he tried his best to avoid eating too many carbs. He knew it was bad enough that he was drinking something as syrupy sweet as red Kool-Aid, so he wasn't about to backslide too far by adding on the potatoes.

He and Semaj sat at the table and ate the same as they did when they were both young boys growing up in the area. Semaj lived in the old wooden three-bedroom house with his grandparents while Rip lived down the street with his aunt who was the sister of Semaj's grandfather. Neither of the boys grew up with their fathers in their lives for different reasons, which caused them to have a kinship that was even tighter than their blood relation.

After they finished eating, Rip realized his cousin needed more time, so instead of pressing him about his father, they spent the rest of the evening reminiscing about all of the fun they had playing tag football in the field down the street. They laughed out loud about the day Rip wrecked his bicycle while riding down the stretch of road that they all called thrill hill. He skinned both knees, his elbow, and even loosened a tooth, but he got back on and they kept on riding.

That type of tenacity was a quality that Rip had never lost over the years. He'd moved to Atlanta in his early twenties and in a few short years he'd become one of the most successful drug dealers in the entire city. At one time he lived in and ruled over Sand Poole Manor as their unofficial king. The residents feared and revered him because of his ruthlessness that had earned him his nickname, which spelled out "rest in peace"; the eventual fate of anyone who dared cross him. During those years, he kept in contact with his best friend and cousin from childhood even though they both lived vastly different lives on opposite sides of the law.

"Do you want to spend the night here?" Semaj asked. They had just finished watching a movie on cable and it was almost eleven at night.

"Sure, why not? I'll stop by the house and see Aunt Jen before we leave tomorrow." He looked intently at his cousin. "We *are* leaving tomorrow, aren't we?"

Semaj nodded his head, then silently walked down the hallway to his bedroom.

Rip went to the hall closet and pulled out a blanket, impressed that things at the house had hardly changed at all since the two of them were young boys. Semaj had purchased some new furniture and a flat-screen TV for the den. He'd also upgraded his bedroom from the bunk beds he'd slept in as a kid to a queen-sized sleigh bed. He'd painted the outside, had new shingles put on the roof, and replaced the air-conditioning unit. However, the majority of the house remained exactly as his grandparents had left it on the day they'd died. The hall closet still contained big fluffy quilts that Semaj's grandma Nettie sewed with her quilting group.

Rip settled comfortably under a quilt on the den couch; then he took out his phone and called Ellen. She didn't pick up so he left her a simple message. "I found Semaj. He's fine, and he'll call you tomorrow," he said. He felt tired from the long drive, and it only took a few moments for him to drift off to sleep and begin snoring loudly.

"Marion, I didn't know you were here too!" Miss Minnie screeched.

Rip slowly opened his eyes realizing that it was early Sunday morning. Miss Minnie stood over him wearing a bright pink flowered dress with a matching huge pink and white hat. He rubbed the sleep from his eyes and sat up.

"Good morning, Miss Minnie. I got here last night. How are you?"

"I'm fine, just fine. You boys better get up or you gonna be late for church."

Rip threw the quilt off of his lap and stood up. "I'm sorry, I didn't bring any church clothes with me this trip. Maybe I'll go next time."

"You can borrow one of my suits," Semaj suggested.

Rip noticed his cousin standing in the doorway dressed in a charcoal grey suit with a black tie and white shirt.

"Um, all right, I guess. Give me a few minutes to get dressed and I'll join you guys."

In their small community the local AME church was only a few miles down the street. After Rip was dressed, he offered to drive both Semaj and Miss Minnie in his Chrysler 300.

"This is a nice car, Marion," Miss Minnie remarked once she was seated in the backseat.

"Thanks, and please call me Rip. I hate being called Marion. That sounds like a woman's name."

"I'm not gonna call you by that awful drug name. I thought you'd left that lifestyle behind you after you got shot," she said.

Feeling reluctant to discuss his past, Rip quickly changed the subject. "Marion is fine, Miss Minnie. I only hear it when I'm home, so I guess I can tolerate it."

After church, Rip was anxious to get back to Atlanta, but he felt Semaj stalling as he made a point to speak to and hug almost every single member of the congregation. When he heard Semaj accept an invitation to dinner with the leader of the Men's Worship group, Rip felt that he had to step in.

"Um, Semaj, you have to go work in the morning so I think we'd better get back to Atlanta. We won't be able to make that dinner."

Semaj looked over at Rip. He didn't want to go back to Atlanta. He wanted to remain in South Carolina around the people who reminded him of his childhood and his home. He wanted to stay there forever and revel in all of the feelings he'd only felt when he was there. But he knew his cousin was right. He was hurt, he felt defeated, but he couldn't hide forever. He knew that he had to go back to Atlanta and go on with his life.

They returned to Semaj's grandparents' house, and after they'd changed clothes and Miss Minnie had gone to her trailer for her Sunday afternoon nap, Semaj asked Rip to sit with him on the back porch because he was finally ready to talk about the day he met his father. When he was done speaking he looked over at Rip for a reaction.

"So this dude who's supposed to be America's favorite dad both on TV and off just looked you in the eyes and lied to you?" Rip asked.

"He sure did. He's such a phony. I remember seeing him on TV after he adopted his oldest son. He went on and on about how much he'd always wanted a son and that he couldn't wait to be a father. He even had the nerve to thank God for blessing him with his son. What a hypocrite."

Rip sat seething with anger at the way his cousin was treated. "So what are you gonna do about it?" he finally asked.

"Nothing. I mean, what can I do about it? I can't force him to be my father. It just really got to me, but I'm good now. I'm heading back to Atlanta later today, and I'll explain everything to Ellen. We'll finish planning the wedding and life will go on."

"I just don't like letting this jerk get away with the way he treated you. You are a grown man with a successful career so he should have known that you didn't come to him looking for money or anything. You just wanted a chance to know your father. That's a right that every man should have, and he stole that from you."

"I understand what you are saying, but—"

"But nothing," Rip said, interrupting him. "My father spent his life behind bars for shooting my mother in a drunken jealous rage. You know that. As horrible as that was, he still wrote me letters from the pen every week until the day he died. If a murdering bastard like that can try to be a real father, then Wayne James at least owes you an explanation."

"You're right, man. You know what I wish? I wish I could just have thirty minutes in a room with just him and me where he couldn't leave, he couldn't deny me, and he'd be forced to explain. Remember that scene from the movie *Uptown at Last* when the wife tied her husband to a chair in the basement to force him to listen to her and answer her questions? That's what I wish I could do to Mr. Wayne James."

Rip listened intently and nodded his head. "I understand perfectly," he said.

"It's getting late. We'd better hit the road. I want to go see Ellen and explain everything before I go home. I'm going to wake up Miss Minnie and let her know I'm leaving."

Rip sat quietly as Semaj walked across the backyard and knocked on Miss Minnie's door. There was a time in his life when he would not have hesitated to put the fear of God into anyone who came close to disrespecting his family the way Wayne James had disrespected Semaj. Even though he'd put that lifestyle behind him, he sat struggling internally as he fought the overwhelming urge to contact some of his former associates and make his cousin's wish come true.

Chapter Six

"Gwen, I'm so glad you could make it," Wayne said. He quickly took off his lapel microphone and rushed over to where she was standing.

"I was surprised when your publicist called. You usually don't like to have family members visit you while you're working," she answered. Gwen stiffened up when he reached out to hug her.

"Hey, what kind of hug was that? We're family, girl." He squeezed her tightly until she finally relaxed and hugged him back. "That's better. I just thought you'd enjoy coming down to the studio and watching me tape my appearance on *The Kandyss Kline Show*. She's nationally syndicated, and I think she's destined to be the next Oprah."

Gwen smiled for the first time since she arrived. "I'm a big fan of hers. I've loved her since she was a member of that eighties girl group Star*shine. Do you think I can get a chance to meet her?"

"Of course. I will personally arrange it. She's in her trailer right now, and I've reserved a spot for you right over there," Wayne pointed to his left. "As soon as the show is over I'll bring you down to chat with her."

Beaming with excitement, Gwen rushed over to the luxurious and comfortable chair Wayne had reserved for her. He'd also arranged for her to receive VIP treatment while she watched the show.

Wayne James was not the only celebrity guest to appear on that day's show. Feeling starstruck, Gwen sat and watched in awe as Kandyss interviewed her favorite rapper, LL Cool J. After his segment, Gwen thought she was going to faint as she watched Shemar Moore step out on stage. She thought he was even more gorgeous in person and felt her heart racing when Shemar took off his shirt and flexed his muscles for the cameras. The last guest to appear before Wayne was Tia Mowry who starred in Gwen's favorite TV show, *The Game.*

As she sat watching her idols she was served an assortment of finger foods and several glasses of champagne. By the end of the show, she was feeling happy, full, and tipsy. So tipsy that she completely forgot to ask Kandyss for an autograph. Instead, she just stared at her with a stupid grin on her face. At Wayne's request, Kandyss was extra polite and friendly and even invited Gwen to come back and watch a live taping of the show whenever she wanted. It didn't matter to Kandyss that it was all a lie because she knew Gwen would never get past security again. When the show was over, Gwen followed Wayne back to his large and lavish dressing room.

"This is so nice. Can I take a picture with my camera phone? Momma has gotta see this. Oh, shoot, I should've taken a picture with Kandyss too. It's too late, isn't it?" Gwen asked.

Wayne chuckled. "I'm afraid so, but I'll ask her to autograph a picture for you when I see her later."

"That would be great," Gwen said, then plopped her ample behind onto the couch. "This is the most comfortable couch I've ever sat on. It feels like a big cloud." She kicked off her shoes and stretched out on the sofa. "You know who else would love to see this?" she said.

"Who?" Wayne asked.

"Semaj, your son. I know things didn't go well last week when I brought him to meet you, but I think you both were just overwhelmed by the whole thing."

Wayne grabbed a chair and pulled it closer to the sofa where Gwen rested. He sat down in front of her. "I'm glad you brought that up, Gwen. You don't really believe that guy was my son, do you?"

"Of course, I believe it, and you should too. I told you before she died your momma told me all about your marriage and your son. It's not just family rumors. Your momma would not lie about something like that."

"You're right, my mother would never lie," Wayne nodded his head in agreement. "Listen, that's one of the reasons I asked you to come by today. We need to talk about what you know and also about this guy, Semaj. He's not my son. I don't know what he told you, but he's not who he claims to be."

Gwen looked at Wayne strangely. "What do you mean?"

"Well, everything my momma told you is the truth. I was a young, rebellious teen, and I ran away from home and got married when I was only eighteen years old. The girl I married was a beautiful young girl named Allison Matthews. We were very immature, and neither of our parents approved of the relationship, but we were very much in love. Shortly after our marriage we had our son, Wayne, Jr. I loved them both with all my heart, but when Wayne, Jr. was just a few months old, our home was destroyed in a tragic fire, and I was left alone and heartbroken."

Sitting up and scooting to the edge of her seat excitedly, Gwen interrupted him. "That's exactly what happened to Semaj's mother. He was pulled out of the fire that his mother died in."

"Gwen, my son, wasn't pulled from the fire. My son died along with his mother." Wayne stared sadly at the floor. "I was at work at my night shift job as a waiter in a diner when it happened, and when I came home, both of them were dead." Dramatically, he paused and wiped away a tear. "Even after all of these years, it's difficult for me to talk about. No one in the family knew the whole story except my mother, and that's how the rumors of my long lost son got started."

"What about all of the things Semaj told me about his mother? The details matched up perfectly."

"He's a reporter, Gwen. Digging into people's backgrounds is what he does for a living. The same way that you were able to research my life story and marriage, he did the same thing."

Gwen sat still on the sofa feeling very confused. She wasn't sure if it was the story that Wayne was telling her or the three glasses of champagne she drank earlier, but the details just did not add up inside her head. "He could not have done what I did. His grandparents changed his name, and he never knew his mother's married name or your name. That's why he's looked for you so long. I had inside family information that helped him out."

Wayne sighed. "Gwen, you told him some things, and he filled in the blanks with his own lies. It's that simple."

Trying to shake off the effects of the alcohol, Gwen sat thinking for several moments before speaking again. "I still don't get it," she finally said. "I mean, what could he possibly gain by pretending to be your son? Semaj is a celebrity."

"I'm one of the richest men in the entertainment industry. This guy is a nightly news anchor on a local television station. He could gain everything by being my son. Things like fame, notoriety, and money mean a lot to people. He could even use my name to advance his own career."

"Wow, I never thought of that. When his cousin asked me to speak to him, I honestly believed that he was being sincere."

"His cousin sent you to him? Gwen, that information should convince you that the whole thing was a setup. Somehow they found out we were related, and unfortunately, they used you to get to me." Wayne turned around and pulled out his briefcase that was sitting on the dressing-room floor. He pulled out a worn newspaper clipping and handed it to Gwen. "During your research, did you happen to find this article?"

Tentatively, Gwen took the paper and read it. Her mouth fell open in surprise when she read the headline. "YOUNG WOMAN AND INFANT SON KILLED IN HOUSE FIRE" She stared at Wayne as she searched for the right words to say. "Wayne, I am so sorry. I was wrong. I was completely wrong. Can you ever forgive me?"

Wayne smile broadly. "Of course, I can, but I need you to do something for me."

"Anything, you just name it," Gwen said. She handed him back the newspaper clipping.

"Let's keep this conversation and our visit with Mr. Matthews between us. I would prefer that none of the rest of the family or anyone knew anything about it."

"I don't understand. Why do we need to keep it a secret?"

Wayne dug down deep and managed to bring up a few more crocodile tears. He reached into his pocket for his handkerchief and wiped them away slowly. "It's really been painful for me to have to bring up the memories of my wife and son. If everyone in the family knew the truth, I'm afraid that I'd have to keep reliving it over and over every time I saw them. Gwen, please don't make me go through that," he pleaded.

Gwen reached out and hugged him tightly. "I'm so sorry. I promise I will not breathe a word of this to anybody. I won't even tell Momma. It will be our secret."

When they broke the embrace Wayne smiled with relief. "If this guy contacts you again, just let me know. I don't think he will bother you, but just in case he tries, I want to know about it."

"I don't think that he will either, but if he does, I promise you that I will handle it. You don't ever have to worry about hearing from him again."

Wayne decided to treat Gwen to lunch, just to make sure that he had cemented her complete trust and loyalty. He told her he'd take her to any restaurant in the city that she picked. He was slightly amused but not at all surprised when she requested to go to Red Lobster. Without making her feel bad about her choice, Wayne convinced her that due to his celebrity status he'd like to take her to the restaurant of one of his personal friends. Her face lit up when he suggested they go to Justin's and perhaps get a chance to see Sean "Puffy" Combs.

As they ate, Wayne reveled in her colorful stories of life in Sand Poole Manor and catching up on all of the latest family gossip. Unlike many celebrities, Wayne did not look down on the members of his family who were still forced to live in low-income neighborhoods, work menial jobs, and live paycheck to paycheck. Wayne realized that without the grace of God, he could have been stuck there just like they were. For that reason, he went out of his way to be sure he kept in close contact with them. Gwen was one of his favorite cousins. She was funny, outgoing, and full of life. For those reasons and many others, he never grew weary of spending time with her. His schedule while in Atlanta was jam-packed with promotional appearances, and he had to admit that had it not been for the situation with Semaj, he would not have had his publicist call her again. He smiled at her across the table realizing that regardless of the circumstances, he was really glad to see her.

While they were eating, Wayne received a call from Kandyss. Due to a timing issue, her producers had advised her that Wayne's segment of the show had been cut in half. They'd been friends for a long time, and she wasn't happy giving him less time than an up-and-coming comedienne would receive. So she'd talked her producers into having a part two and allowing him to appear on her show for two days. She asked him to return to the studio, and with a change of clothes and the magic of editing, it would appear that he was there for two shows.

Wayne excused himself from lunch and called Doug to come to the restaurant and give Gwen a ride home. He rushed back to the studio and returned to his dressing room to wait for the second taping to begin. He chose a powder-blue three-piece suit from his vast collection, matched it up with a striped tie, and sat down to wait for the makeup girl to arrive.

While he waited, he realized it was almost four o'clock so he turned on the television to catch up on the local news. He flipped casually through the channels until he saw Semaj's face on the screen talking about a multiple shooting that had occurred on the city's east side. In spite of himself, Wayne beamed with pride. As he watched, he couldn't help but notice that Semaj had inherited Allison's high cheekbones, thick eyebrows, and dazzling smile. Semaj's teeth were perfectly straight and white, just like his mother's had been. "You have her smile, but those are definitely my eyes," Wayne said to television.

Chapter Seven

Ellen sat quietly on her sister's living-room sofa flipping through a magazine while Aaliyah stared at the television. She'd been watching the same DVD over and over again all afternoon, but Ellen didn't mind. She was grateful for anything that would keep her quiet and occupied.

When Ellen arrived at the hospital the previous weekend, she'd found out that her sister had suffered a mild concussion. Although Jenise denied it, Ellen knew it was the result of Reggie's latest beating. The doctors questioned her repeatedly and even had a social worker come in to speak with her, but Jenise still would not admit that her head injury was caused by her husband's fist slamming into her head over and over again. Ellen had hoped that the police would be called and charges would be filed against Reggie, but as long as Jenise refused to cooperate, there was very little that they could do.

As a condition of her release, the doctor had advised that Jenise should not be left alone, and that she needed to be observed for the next several days to make sure she didn't black out once again. They arrived at her apartment in the wee hours of the morning on that Sunday and realized that Reggie was gone. Ellen felt relieved and immediately agreed to stay with her sister for as long as she needed her.

It had been a week, and although Reggie had not returned, Jenise was feeling much better and had not had any episodes of confusion or dizziness for a few days. Ellen had made up her mind that if everything went well with her sister's health for the rest of the day, she would return to her home after church on Sunday.

"Auntie Ellen, can I watch it again?" Aaliyah asked.

Ellen looked up from her magazine and suddenly noticed that the DVD had ended.

"Are you sure you don't want to watch something else?" she asked. "You've watched this one all day."

"*Shrek* is my favorite. Please can I watch it one more time?"

No matter how hard she tried, Ellen could not resist her niece's beautiful brown eyes when they were peering up at her, pleading. "Of course, you can, honey. I'm going to fix dinner so that it will be ready when your mom wakes up from her nap."

"Sketti, sketti," Aaliyah squealed.

Ellen laughed. "No, we had spaghetti last night. How about we have chicken fingers and broccoli with lots of cheese sauce?"

"Yay," Aaliyah cheered happily.

Ellen started the DVD once again for her niece, then went into the kitchen to cook dinner. She took the chicken fingers from the refrigerator and after washing them thoroughly, she seasoned and battered them before placing them on a pan that she put into the oven to cook. Next, she boiled some water on the stove and placed the basket full of broccoli over it to steam. She went back to the living room to check on Aaliyah; then she grabbed her magazine and returned to the kitchen. She was sitting at the table waiting for the food to get done when she heard the sound of a key in the front-door lock.

"Daddy!" she heard Aaliyah say.

"Hey, baby girl, where's your mommy? Is she cooking dinner? Something sure smells good in here." Reggie walked into the kitchen and was surprised to see Ellen scowling at him with her arms folded across her chest. "Oh, it's you. What are you doing here, Ellen?"

"I picked your wife up from the hospital last week, and the doctor said that she couldn't be alone. I've been here all week. Where have *you* been?"

Reggie turned his back to her and walked toward the bedroom. "None of your business," he yelled over his shoulder.

"Reggie, wait a minute. I need to talk to you."

"Can't it wait? I want to see if my wife is okay."

Ellen walked into the living room behind him. "No, it can't wait. I need to talk to you about something important before you see her."

"What is it now, Ellen?" he asked with an annoyed tone.

Glancing down at Aaliyah who was engrossed in the television, Ellen turned toward the kitchen. "Can we talk in there?" she asked.

Reluctantly, Reggie followed her back into the kitchen. He pulled out a chair and slumped down into it. "Make it quick," he ordered.

Ellen sat down across from him and carefully chose her words. "Look, I know that you will not admit it, but you are the reason my sister is lying back there with a mild concussion."

Reggie opened his mouth to protest, but Ellen interrupted him and held up her hand.

"Like I said, I know you won't admit it, and I really don't care if you do or not. I know what I know. The reason I'm talking to you is because regardless of how you treat her, for whatever reason, my sister loves you."

A smug smile spread across Reggie's face. "Yeah, she does," he said.

"If you love her too, then I'm asking you. No, I'm pleading with you to please stop using her for a punching bag. My sister is a beautiful woman, and no matter what you are going through with your music career, she does not deserve your wrath." Ellen turned and reached into her purse. She pulled out a piece of paper and unfolded it. "My church has a domestic violence class. It's for couples like you and Jenise. They teach you how to control your anger and turn to God when you are stressed out rather than lashing out at each other. I know that you believe in God; you sing about Him. All I'm asking is that you and Jenise attend these classes. You need help. You both need it."

Reggie snatched the paper from her hands and crumpled it up. "I don't need to go to no domestic violence classes. Me and Jenise are just fine. Besides, if I went to those classes, it would ruin my career before it started. How can I go into churches in this area and minister my music if they think I've been hitting my wife? Forget it!"

"How can you go into churches in this community and minister your music when you *know* that you hit your wife?" Ellen asked.

"Stay outta our business, Ellen." Reggie pointed a long, skinny finger at her face. "What goes on between me and Jenise is none of your business. You got that?"

Ellen sighed loudly. "Yeah, I got it." She stood up from the table and went over to the stove to check on dinner.

"Leave that and I'll finish cooking. I'm glad you stayed with Jenise while I was away, but I'm home now, so you can get your stuff and bounce.".

Ellen glared at him and was just about to refuse to leave when Jenise walked into the kitchen. Her eyes lit up like a lightning bug when she saw Reggie. "Baby, when did you get home?" she asked. She reached down and hugged him tightly.

"I just got here a few minutes ago," he said, hugging her back. "Why didn't you tell me what the doctor said when I called last week?"

Jenise pulled out a chair and sat beside him. She glanced over at her sister before answering. "I didn't want to worry you while you were working in the studio at your mom's house. Besides, Ellen didn't mind staying here, did you, Sissy?" she asked.

Although she didn't mind staying with her sister at all Ellen was livid to find out that her sister had been in contact with Reggie and had not told him what was going on. When she'd asked about him, Jenise had pretended that she had no idea where he'd gone or when he'd be back. As much as she loved her sister, Ellen was growing weary of the lies she constantly told to protect her husband.

"Listen, since Reggie is here, I'm gonna go ahead and go home." She gave Jenise a quick hug, then left them alone in the kitchen. Her stomach did flip-flops as she heard the two of them laughing and giggling with each other like teenagers. Ellen was aware that there were many times when Reggie was very affectionate and loving toward her sister, but in her mind, those times did not outweigh the multiple times that he treated her as if she was less than a stray dog he'd found wandering in the street. No matter what anyone said, that wasn't her idea of what love was all about.

She went into Aaliyah's bedroom that she had shared with her for the past week and grabbed her overnight bag and threw her things randomly into it. On her way out the door she gave her niece a big hug and a kiss. "Do you remember when I showed you how to call nine-one-one?" she asked her niece.

"I do, Auntie Ellen," she answered.

"What's my phone number?"

Aaliyah grinned and recited the number proudly, "404-555-0988."

"That's perfect. Now if you ever need anything you can call me, or you can call nine-one-one if there's a problem. Do you understand?"

Aaliyah nodded her little head, and her ponytails bobbed back and forth.

Ellen went to the door, then instructed Aaliyah to lock it securely after she was gone. As she descended the staircase on her way to the parking lot, she began to fervently pray.

"Dear Lord, please take care of my sister and my niece. Protect them, Lord. Keep them both safe from hurt, harm, or danger. Touch my sister's heart and open her eyes. Help her to see through the love she feels and protect her and her child. In Jesus' name I pray, amen."

Since it was still early in the evening Ellen decided against going straight home. Instead, she dialed Semaj's number and asked if he wouldn't mind having some company.

"You know you can come by here anytime," he said as he smiled into the phone.

"Have you had dinner yet? I can stop and pick up something for both of us," she suggested.

"No, you don't have to do that. I'll order from Von-nie's Soul Food, and the delivery should be here by the time you arrive. What do you want me to order for you?"

Maneuvering through traffic Ellen tried to quickly remember what her favorite dish was from Vonnie's. "I think I'm in the mood for barbeque ribs and a baked sweet potato," she said finally.

"That sounds delicious. I think I'll order the same. See you soon, sweetheart. I love you," Semaj said before hanging up the phone.

Ellen felt relieved that he finally seemed to be in a good mood. Although he'd apologized for his disappearing act the previous week, Ellen couldn't help but still feel concerned about the entire situation. In all honesty, she felt the excuse he'd given her was just plain lame. When he finally called after not answering his phone for four days, he'd told Ellen that he was homesick so he went back to South Carolina for a few days. He told her that a story he was working on had triggered some memories of his grandparents, and he just felt the need to be inside their home and around their things until the feeling passed. When she'd asked what story, he told her it was a story about an elderly couple just like his grandparents who'd passed away following a bad car accident on the same day. While the story somewhat mirrored what had happened in his family, Ellen knew that he covered similar stories all the time and he'd never acted that way before. Since that time he'd been different. She couldn't put her finger on exactly what it was, but she was sure that he simply wasn't acting like himself any longer.

Semaj had been moody since the day they'd met. Ellen had often joked that he had more mood swings than a pregnant woman. One minute he was happy and acting like he was on the top of the world, and the next, he'd be melancholy and sad. They'd discussed it with their pastor during their premarital counseling sessions, and the pastor had chalked it all up to Semaj's tragic loss of his grandparents at such a young age. She'd learned to live with it, and it had actually become a part of his charm. She was also a loner by nature, so if he wasn't in the best mood, she'd use that time to do things for herself. But the mood he'd been in for the past week was way beyond anything she'd ever experienced with him before. He wasn't sad or mad, and he didn't seem annoyed or even downhearted. If she had to give it a name, she'd have to say that he simply acted lost. It was as if he was behind a brick wall and couldn't find his way out.

The delivery driver for Vonnie's Soul Food pulled into the parking lot of Semaj's apartments at the same time as Ellen, and they walked to the door together while she savored the smell of the ribs. As Semaj paid the driver, she went into the kitchen to look for drinks. As usual, Semaj had several bottles of his favorite soft drink in the fridge. She took two glasses from the cabinet, filled them with ice, and poured them both full of Mountain Dew Code Red. She took them into the dining room and sat down at the table. Semaj came over and set the plates of food down in front of them. Without a word he sat down beside her and grabbed her hand. Ellen knew that was his way of asking her to say grace. She blessed the food, and then the two of them dug in.

"These ribs are delicious," Semaj mumbled in between bites. "It's too bad Vonnie doesn't cater. I'd love to have her food for our wedding reception."

"Speaking of our wedding reception, we need to set up an appointment with Cedric to taste the menu selections for the reception," Ellen said.

Semaj wiped barbeque sauce from his face. "Are you sure we can afford this guy? I know he's a friend of yours, but I'm worried that even with the discount, it's going to break the bank."

"Oh, that's right. I didn't tell you. Do you remember the little girl you found last year named Cyndi?"

"Of course, I do. Some idiot crackhead tried to sell her for a hit. Rip used his connections to help me find her."

Ellen grinned eagerly, "Well, that little girl was Cedric's sister. After he found out who I am marrying, he insisted that he cater the wedding for us absolutely free."

Semaj stared at her in disbelief. "Are you kidding me? He actually said that it's free?"

"Yes. I told him that you love what you do and that you are not in it for the money, but he didn't care. He said that he wanted to bless us. I couldn't say no to a blessing."

Semaj's cell phone began vibrating on the table. He checked the caller ID and saw his cousin's name. "Do you mind if I answer that?" he asked.

"Go ahead, I'm done eating so I'm just going to throw these containers away and straighten up the kitchen."

Semaj picked up the phone and walked down the hallway into his bedroom. "Hey, man, what's up?" he asked.

"It's not Christmas or your birthday, but I'm your fairy godfather," Rip answered. "Your wish is my command."

"You're my *what?*"

Rip began to sing loudly off-key. "*When you wish upon a star, makes no difference what you are, up above the world so high . . .*" He suddenly stopped. "Wait a minute, that's not right," he said and laughed loudly.

Semaj began laughing hysterically as well. He didn't quite understand, but his cousin's singing was so bad it cracked him up. When the laughing finally died down

Semaj decided to ask him again what he was talking about. "So you say you are a fairy and you like to sing too?" he joked.

"I'm not Tinker Bell, but I can grant wishes and with my help, your wish is about to come true."

"What are you talking about? What wish?"

"Do you remember when we were in South Carolina last week and you said that you wished you could have a few minutes alone with that jerk Wayne James?"

Semaj closed his bedroom door to make sure that Ellen would not overhear their conversation. "Of course, I remember. You didn't call him, did you? I told you that I didn't want to have anything to do with that guy."

"Man, you haven't heard the latest. I talked to Gwen, and she said that he told her that you were a big fat liar. He told her that there was no way you could be his son because his son is dead. He told Gwen you were a con artist after his money. Can you believe that crap?"

"He said his son is dead? Are you sure about that?"

"Of course, I'm sure. He even showed Gwen some phony newspaper clipping with a fake headline saying that his son died in the fire with his wife. Then he told Gwen not to tell anybody about you or their conversation, but you know me. I coaxed it out of her. As if it wasn't bad enough that he lied to your face, now he's telling lies on you behind your back. That's the last straw. Don't worry about the details. Just know that your cousin is going to make sure that you get your wish."

Suddenly realizing exactly what he meant, Semaj slowly sat down on his bed. "Rip, you are on probation, man. You can't risk your freedom for me. Whatever you are thinking about, just forget it."

"I can't forget it. This guy treated you like gutter trash, and that is unacceptable. Besides, I wouldn't even have my freedom if it wasn't for you. I owe you, Semaj, and you know that I always pay my debts."

The sound of Ellen knocking at the door distracted Semaj momentarily from the conversation. "Yeah, honey, what is it?" he called out.

"Do you want some ice cream? I was just about to fix some for myself."

"No, I'm good."

Before speaking again he waited until he heard her footsteps return to the kitchen. When he heard the refrigerator door opening he returned to the conversation. "Rip, listen, I appreciate what you want to do, but this is not the way. Wayne James is just not worth it." Semaj paused and waited for an answer. "Rip, are you there?" He repeated his name several more times, but he knew it was no use. His cousin had already hung up.

"Don't stop him. Revenge is sweet," a voice said. Semaj looked to his left and just like in the movies he could've sworn he saw a miniature replica of himself in a red suit with horns and a tail sitting on his shoulder. The little devil spoke again. *"Wayne James treated you like crap. All you wanted was to know him. You didn't deserve to be treated that way."*

Semaj nodded his head in agreement. "You're right. He deserves whatever Rip is planning to do to him. Why should I care?"

"He's your father. You have to forgive him," another voice said.

Semaj looked to his right and saw another tiny version of himself. This one was dressed all in white with a golden halo. For a few moments he wondered if he was freaking out as he watched the two arguing back and forth. The devil pointed out once again how badly Semaj had been treated by his father, while the little angel pleaded with Semaj to turn the other cheek. Finally unable to listen to the debate any longer, Semaj reached up and smacked the little angel off of his shoulder. He watched in silence as he vividly tumbled to the floor and landed with a loud thud. Stepping over him, Semaj opened his bedroom door and returned to the living room.

"Hey, Ellen, I've changed my mind. I think I will have some ice cream after all."

Chapter Eight

Rip gulped down the last swallow of his third Red Bull, then threw the can out of the window of the van. A part of him was afraid of what he was about to do, but another part believed that it was the only thing that he could do.

For most of his adult life, Rip had lived and breathed crime. Every thought, word, or deed that he committed was the result of trying to get over and find the easiest way to get paid, regardless of the legalities of the activity. The only law or code that he lived by was the code of the streets, and that code dictated that he could not allow Wayne to get away with disrespecting Semaj.

Rip's first brush with the law occurred when he was only fourteen years old. He and Semaj had walked to the corner store to buy snacks while on summer vacation. Semaj's grandparents were considered to be one of the more well-to-do families in the neighborhood, and they always made sure that he had pocket money. Rip, on the other hand, lived with his elderly aunt whose only source of income was welfare, food stamps, and anything she could beg from social services, the community food bank, or her family members.

The two of them went inside the store, and Semaj picked out a Pepsi from the cooler and a bag of potato chips and a MoonPie off the shelf. Then he went to the counter to pay. Rip followed him and picked up the same items. While the clerk was distracted with ringing up Semaj's purchases, Rip had shoved all of his items into his backpack, and then he tried to run out of the store. Unfortunately, the store owner's wife had seen everything, and she used a broom to trip him up just as he reached the front door. He fell headfirst to the ground, and everything he'd stolen went tumbling down with him. It was only petty theft, but the racist judge that Rip stood before in the backwoods town of Andrus, South Carolina, sentenced him to two years in a juvenile detention facility.

Bad behavior, a bad attitude, and an assault on another inmate resulted in Rip spending the remainder of his teen years behind bars. He was released three days after his eighteenth birthday. His aunt Jenn that had raised him allowed him to stay with her for a few months, but working a regular job in the slow Southern town did not appeal to him. He contacted Semaj in Atlanta and asked if he could join him.

The two cousins shared a small apartment in the SWATS area of Atlanta. Semaj spent his days going to classes at Morris Brown College and his nights working various odd jobs to make ends meet. Rip spent his days sleeping and his nights hustling, robbing, and finding new and inventive ways to con people out of their hard earned money. By the time Semaj had graduated from college and began working for the local TV station as a field reporter, Rip had built a small drug empire. He loved his cousin, but he also realized that their lives were going in vastly different directions. Partly for Semaj's protection and also partly for the convenience of his business, Rip moved out of their apartment after paying one of his many female companions to rent an apartment for him in Sand Poole Manor. Throughout the years, he kept in contact with his cousin, while also keeping a safe distance.

Rip was born a pudgy baby that grew into chubby child, a fat teen, and then a morbidly obese man. Although he rarely saw a doctor or stood on a calibrated scale, Rip was sure that his weight ballooned to well over 400 pounds at one point. During this time, he'd begun to rule his empire at Sand Poole from the comfort and security of his apartment. He believed that he had enough cops on his payroll to ensure that he and anyone who worked for him was safe from prosecution, and for a very long time he lived with a false sense of happiness.

The people who were Rip's customers and associates would probably explain what happened in his life next as fate, or maybe even Karma, but Rip knew in his heart that it was nothing but God. One night as Rip was lounging in his bed alone watching his favorite movie *Scarface*, a swarm of DEA agents kicked in his front door. Rip reached for the 9 mm gun that he kept under his mattress, but it was too late. The agents began firing rounds, and Rip was hit twelve times. Many were just superficial wounds, but the most crucial bullet lodged in his spine as he tried to turn to get away. Rip woke up a week later unable to feel his legs with a DEA agent standing over his bed asking questions. A few feet away from the bed Rip saw his cousin Semaj and his aunt Jenn with tears streaming down her face.

Up until that point, Rip couldn't remember ever praying in his entire life. He'd been brought up in a Christian home, but he'd never accepted the prayers or the faith that his aunt possessed. Yet at that moment in time, Rip instinctively knew that he'd reach the point of no return. Ignoring the agent and his questions, he closed his eyes and prayed.

"God, I can't feel my legs. I know that after the things I've done and said I don't deserve to ask you for anything. I'm not worthy of your love, but I can feel it all over me. Lord, I swear to you, if you let me walk again, I will turn my life around and never commit another crime. I will tell this agent everything that he wants to know, and even if I end up walking around a prison yard, I am pleading with you to please, just let me walk again."

When he was done praying Rip lapsed into unconsciousness again. He awoke several days later, and al-

though he still could not feel his legs, he had faith that
as long as he kept his promise, God would heal him. The
first step in that promise was speaking to the DEA agents
regarding his business. Due to his physical condition and
Semaj's uptown attorney's influence, the agent offered
him a deal. Rip turned state's evidence and completely
avoided doing any jail time. Instead, he received a sus-
pended sentence of ten years, along with six years probation in exchange for his testimony. Fourteen months and
five surgeries later, he took his first footstep, and many
others followed after that. He spent another six months
doing rehab and almost two years after the incident
he was finally able to walk out of the hospital over 150
pounds lighter.

He returned to Sand Poole Manor, but he no longer
had a three-bedroom pimped out luxury apartment.
Instead, he rented a modest one-bedroom apartment
that he was able to pay for with the money he received
from disability payments. He wasn't the king anymore,
but he still commanded a huge amount of respect from
his neighbors and friends. With Semaj's assistance,
he'd enrolled in classes online and was looking forward
to earning a degree in computer science. He attended
church regularly and truly felt that he'd kept his promise to God. He was a changed man, and there was no
temptation for him to go back to his former life.

That was, until Wayne James had entered the picture and totally disrespected the one person who
meant more to Rip than anyone else in the world. He
knew he'd never break the law again for money, but
this was a matter of honor. He had no intention of
harming Wayne, but he was determined to make sure
that he took time out of his busy celebrity schedule to
listen to whatever his cousin felt the need to say.

Matters of the heart were foreign to Rip. Due to his
lifestyle, he'd never had one steady girlfriend. He instead usually kept a stable of lovelies that he could call

on at any time. Since he'd first seen her wide hips wiggling across the courtyard at Sand Poole Manor, Gwen had found her way to the top of his long list of conquests. Rip really liked her, but in order to accomplish his task, he'd had to resort to manipulating her for information. It wasn't difficult because Gwen loved to talk, and no subject was off-limits when her tongue began to wag, but he still felt a twinge of guilt for using her.

Currently, he was sitting in a borrowed utility van outside of the condo Gwen had told him that Wayne rented for the duration of his stay in Atlanta. He'd chosen to leave the hotel when he realized that instead of being in town for three weeks, he'd probably be there for three months. He'd signed a short-term lease on a furnished condo and leased a new Cadillac to drive around the city in. Gwen had also been forthcoming with his full schedule as well as that of Doug's. Gwen's gossipy nature was the final piece to the puzzle. It allowed Rip the opportunity to strike when Wayne was alone and vulnerable. Now it was just a matter of time before he would descend the stairs and Rip's plan would commence.

Two hours later, Rip removed the blindfold that had been surrounding Wayne's face and blocking his vision. He was seated in a hard wooden chair, his hands were bound behind his back, and his feet were tied tightly to the chair legs. After untying the blindfold, Rip bent down and reached for the ropes, and then he tightened them, making sure that Wayne could barely move.

"Who are you, and what do you want from me?" Wayne screamed into the darkness. Rip refused to answer, and Wayne's voice echoed, then faded into silence.

Rip wanted to make things as simple as possible, and for that reason, he had not spoken a word since he'd grabbed Wayne from behind just as he was exiting his condo. Wayne was about to get into his car when a gun was poked into his back. He calmly cooperated and offered his wallet to Rip, but he didn't want his money or Wayne's brand-new slate-blue Cadillac Escalade. He wanted Wayne, and he quickly blindfolded, bound, and gagged him, then threw him into the back of the utility van. They drove around for a while. Rip retraced his route several times, and he grappled with his conscience. At one point, he considered abandoning the whole plan and taking Wayne back, but he realized he was in too deep now and had to continue.

Finally, Rip pulled into the parking lot of an abandoned warehouse and stopped the van. He jumped out of the front seat and walked around the back to open the door. He reached in and grabbed his victim and dragged him forward with his arms pinned tightly behind his back. Rip grabbed the large sliding garage door, and it screeched loudly as it opened, and then he closed it behind them.

"I'm hungry. Aren't you at least going to feed me?" Wayne screamed.

"Later," Rip answered in a gruff voice.

"Please, can I at least have some water? It's hot in here, and I'm thirsty."

Without a word Rip kneeled down and opened a blue cooler he'd brought in and set on the warehouse floor. He reached inside and pulled out a bottle of water, then he opened it as he walked toward Wayne. "Open your mouth," he instructed.

Obediently, Wayne complied, and the cool liquid trickled into his mouth and down his throat. When he'd had enough, he turned his head to prevent Rip from pouring more in. "Thank you," he said into the darkness.

"I need to go make a phone call. Make yourself comfortable, and I promise to bring you something to eat when I come back," Rip said.

"Wait, don't go. Just tell me what you want with me. If it's money, I have at least four hundred in cash in my wallet, and I can get more."

"I don't want your money, and I'm not going to hurt you. Just relax and sit tight. Everything will be clear to you very soon."

Rip opened the garage door and left Wayne alone in the darkness. Once outside, he pulled out his cell phone and called Semaj.

"It's done," he said as soon as Semaj picked up.

Semaj turned to Ellen who was seated beside him on the sofa. "I'll be right back, baby, this is a business call," he lied. He walked out of the apartment and closed the door behind him, then walked down the stairs to the parking lot before speaking again to be sure that no one overheard him.

"I just got a call from the newsroom asking me to come in and cover a breaking news story regarding America's favorite TV dad, Wayne James, who was abducted from the parking lot of his condo. Please, Rip, tell me that you didn't have anything to do with that."

"You know the answer to that question, man."

Semaj sighed. "I do, but I was sincerely hoping that I was wrong. Kidnapping is a felony, Rip. If you're caught, it will violate your probation, and you will go to jail for a very long time. I appreciate your loyalty, but this was a mistake—a big, big mistake."

"If anyone made a mistake it was Wayne James when he decided that he was too good to acknowledge you as his son. This creep adopted five orphans and gave them a beautiful home in the Hollywood Hills, lavished them with gifts, and they've enjoyed the kind of life most people only dream of. He's on television week after week spouting lines about fatherhood that the entire country imitates. This fool even has a book on the *New York Times* Bestsellers list called *The Joys of Fatherhood*. Gwen told me that he's in Atlanta now because Tyler Perry is interested in turning his books into a movie. Yet this poor excuse for a man couldn't take five minutes with his own seed? That's trifling."

Semaj wanted to scream, "You're absolutely right" at the top of his lungs. Rip was saying the words that had tumbled around in his head ever since the day Gwen took him to Wayne's hotel. It just didn't make sense. Semaj admired Wayne James and had even once fantasized about having a father just like him. His grandfather had done the best that he could, but in his soul, Semaj longed for his dad. In his heart, he knew what Rip had done was five kinds of wrong, but he suddenly did not care.

"Where is he? Is he okay?" Semaj asked.

"Yeah, he's fine. I got him tied up in the warehouse where I used to keep my products back in the day. When I left he was whining about being hungry."

"So he's all alone?"

"Yep, I was going to get him a sandwich or something."

Semaj looked around the parking lot to be sure that no one was watching or listening to him. "All right, here's the plan. Take him a sandwich, feed him, then leave him there for the night. I've got to get to the station to cover the story, and I'll get back to you about our next move tomorrow."

"So you're in with me?" Rip asked.

"I'm all in," Semaj said.

As Semaj walked back up the stairs to his apartment a grin spread across his face as he thought of his father sitting alone in the darkness feeling abandoned and neglected, just as his absence had made Semaj feel for his entire life.

Chapter Nine

"How do I look?" Jenise asked as she stepped out of the dressing room of the bridal salon wearing her emerald-green bridesmaid's dress. For her sister who was also the matron of honor, Ellen had chosen a strapless chiffon dress with a layered knee-length skirt that showed off her sister's gorgeous athletic legs. Jenise twirled around to give Ellen a better view.

"You look absolutely beautiful," Ellen answered. "Maybe I don't need to have you as my matron of honor after all. You're going to upstage me as the bride," she teased.

"That will never happen. You have always been the pretty one. You know I'm the family ugly duckling." Jenise turned to her left side and looked closer at herself in the mirror.

It broke Ellen's heart when her sister said things like that. They were both very pretty, but her sister had never believed that she was, and Ellen did not understand why. They both had long, thick hair that reminded people of the actress Shari Headley. Jenise was five feet seven while Ellen was only five feet six. Each of them had slim, shapely bodies, and neither struggled with their weight. By most standards, they were both considered extremely beautiful. The only real difference in how the two sisters looked was that Jenise was much darker than Ellen. This had caused her to be the butt of a lot of teasing when they children. It was always Ellen who was what was considered as light bright, who had to jump in and defend her sister whenever the kids referred to her as chocolate drop or darkie. Jenise would hide her face and run home in tears.

Over the years, Ellen and their parents had tried their best to convince Jenise that she was beautiful no matter what shade her skin was, but Ellen realized that the teasing had deeply affected her self-esteem. She also felt that it was probably the reason that Ellen married a man who was physically abusive. For some reason, her sister didn't believe she deserved any better.

"Jenise, you are not ugly. You are very beautiful," Ellen said to reassure her.

"Girl, you are gorgeous," the salesgirl said, chiming in. "I wish I had your figure. I'd have men lined up taking numbers."

Jenise looked at her and blushed. "Thank you," she said. "I know I have a banging body, but it's this face that needs a bag over it." She put her hands on her hips and posed in the mirror again.

"Please, your face is gorgeous too," the salesgirl answered. "If I didn't know better, I'd think you were Gabrielle Union's sister. You look a lot like her, you know."

When Ellen saw her sister blushing even more she was grateful to see that she finally seemed to be accepting of a genuine compliment.

"Can I try on my dress today too, Auntie Ellen?" Aaliyah said. She was seated beside Ellen dangling her little legs off the chair. "I wanna look pretty like Mommy."

"No, sweetie, your dress fits just fine. We don't need you to put it on again. You'll look just as pretty as your mommy on the wedding day," Ellen answered.

Jenise finally stopped looking at herself at the mirror and turned toward the dressing room. "Let me get this off, Sissy, and then we can go over to Cedric's for the food tasting. Are you sure you want me to do this with you? I mean, it really should be your fiancé."

"I know, and I really wish that Semaj could do it, but he's been busy at work with the whole Wayne James case for the last week."

Jenise noticed the worried look on her sister's face. "Is everything all right with you two, Sissy?"

Ellen looked at her sister, then moved her eyes in Aaliyah's direction. Their sisterly vibe allowed Jenise to realize that she did not want to talk about it in front of her niece. "Everything's fine," she lied.

Jenise knowingly nodded her head, then walked back into the dressing room to take off the dress. She emerged a few moments later and handed it to the salesgirl to bag for them. Then she walked over to where her sister and daughter were sitting.

"Aaliyah, how would you like to spend the rest of the afternoon with your Nanna?" she said.

Both Ellen and Aaliyah stared at her in surprise.

"Can I please?" Aaliyah asked.

It wasn't often that Aaliyah spent time with her maternal grandparents. Because of the fact that both of her parents were well aware that Reggie was abusive, it had caused a huge rift in their relationship. Her father refused to come to their home, and he made it clear that Reggie was not welcome in his. Jenise's loyalty kept her from visiting her parents' home without him, where she knew that she'd be bombarded with constant criticisms of the man she loved.

"If you bring that sorry son of a biscuit eater to my house, I swear I won't be responsible for my actions," her father had said once.

Malcolm Winston was a deacon in his church, and he did his best to find new and colorful ways not to curse.

However, he had been overly protective of his daughters their entire lives, and they all knew that he would not hesitate to do whatever it took to protect them.

Their mother, Deloris, was the eternal peacekeeper. If her husband was not with her she would sneak over to Jenise's apartment and spend a few moments with them. Her visits never lasted long, however, as she didn't want to lie to her husband about her whereabouts. Many times after she was gone, Jenise would find money tucked under a candy dish or in Aaliyah's underwear drawer, and she knew that her mother was doing her best to be there for them without upsetting their father.

"I called Mom from the dressing room. She's going to meet us at the front of the mall to pick up Aaliyah and take her to McDonald's for a Happy Meal. That way, you and I can take our time with Cedric at the tasting."

"You didn't have to do that. I don't mind bringing Aaliyah along with us."

Jenise put her arm around her sister's shoulder as she stood up to leave. "I know you don't, Sissy, but I also know that you need to talk. Besides, you know that little munchkin of mines loves chicken nuggets." She smiled and winked at Jenise.

The mall was packed with patrons on a Saturday afternoon, so by the time they paid for the dress and maneuvered their way to the front entrance, their mother's car was sitting idling at the curb. Jenise walked over to open the passenger door for Aaliyah and suddenly noticed that her father was sitting there.

"Daddy? I didn't know you were coming too," she said surprised.

Malcolm opened the door of the car and hopped out. "I haven't seen my granddaughter since Christmas. Your mother assured me that Reggie was not with you

so I decided to come along. I hope you don't mind."
He bent down and picked Aaliyah up into his massive
arms and hugged her tightly.

"Hey, Poppa! Can we get some ice cream?" Aaliyah
asked. She put her little arms tightly around his neck.

"You can have anything you want, Pumpkin," he answered.

"Dad, you know I don't mind you spending time
with her. I'm really glad to see you too." Jenise hugged
her dad around his free arm that did not contain her
daughter.

Malcolm opened the back passenger door and put
Aaliyah in while Jenise walked around to the driver's
side to talk with her mother.

After Malcolm had Aaliyah secured in her seat belt,
he closed the door and turned toward Ellen. She was
staring out into the parking lot as if lost in thought.
"Are you all right, Ellen?" he asked.

She turned and looked in his direction as if she'd
just noticed that he was there. "Dad? Yes, I'm fine,"
she answered. She leaned down and looked over at her
mother. "Hi, Mommy, you look nice today." She plastered a fake smile on her face.

Her mother's intuition kicked in as soon as she
looked into Ellen's face. Deloris noticed that she looked
exhausted, and she was sure that her smile was not
genuine. "Are you sure you're okay, honey? You look a
little tired. Are you getting enough rest?"

"I'm fine, Mommy. It's just prewedding jitters. Please
don't worry about me." Ellen tried to make her smile
look more authentic.

Deloris was not convinced, but she decided not to
push it. "All right then. You call me if you need any help
with anything, okay?"

"I will, Mommy. I promise."

Her mother turned her attention toward Jenise and lowered her voice. "Find out what's going on with her and you can tell me when I drop off Aaliyah later."

Jenise nodded her head, then leaned in and kissed her mother on the cheek. "Thanks for keeping Aaliyah today. I really appreciate it."

On the ride across town to Cedric's catering company Jenise could tell that her sister's mind was a million miles away. She tried her best to lighten the mood. "Hey, guess who I ran into at the grocery store yesterday."

"I don't know, who?" Ellen asked indifferently.

"Butterbean," Jenise said, then doubled over in the seat laughing.

In spite of her bad mood, Ellen could not help laughing too. "Butterbean Logan?" she asked.

"Do you know any other Butterbeans? Of course I mean Butterbean Logan."

The two of them continued laughing hysterically as they headed through Atlanta.

Butterbean Logan was a guy Ellen had met from an online dating service years before she began dating Semaj. Although she'd dated in high school and had one or two boyfriends in college, Ellen had not met anyone whom she felt she could get serious with. Her biological clock was ticking as she inched closer to thirty so she had decided to sign up with the online dating site called Soulmates.com. It turned out to be the one of the most interesting, comical, and horrible dates of her life.

On the night of their date, Ellen was inside her apartment checking her makeup in the mirror one last time when she heard the doorbell ring. She took a long, deep breath and walked to the front door. She peered out of the peephole, but didn't see anyone.

I must be hearing things, she thought to herself before returning to the bathroom to brush her hair a bit more.

A few minutes later, the doorbell rang again so Ellen returned to the front door and peeped out once more. She still did not see anyone. As she stood peering through the peephole she thought she noticed a shadow in the darkness of the breezeway, and she heard someone knocking at the door. Frightened, she stepped back and called out.

"Who is it?" she yelled.

"I'm your date. Butterbean Logan."

Tentatively, Ellen grabbed the doorknob and pulled the door open and looked down. Standing before her she recognized the handsome face of the man she'd been speaking to online for the past three weeks before setting a date. However, she was sure that he'd stolen the body of a ten-year-old boy. At five foot six, Ellen had not met many men who were shorter than she, but Butterbean was the exception. Even with the lifts he later told her were in his shoes, he still only stood at five foot two.

Any physical attraction that she'd felt online instantly dissipated into thin air, and she seriously considered slamming the door in his face until she realized that would not be the Christian thing to do. Instead, she put on a bogus smile and grabbed her purse so that they could go out to dinner.

In the parking lot she expected him to walk over to a small Toyota or maybe even a Honda as his car. She was shocked when he stepped up to a shiny white Hummer and clicked the auto unlock on his key chain. He politely walked Ellen to her side of the truck, and when the door opened, a custom, three-stair ladder fell down.

"Climb in," he said.

Ellen did as he said, and then waited while he walked around and climbed up on his customer ladder.

As if reading her mind he began to explain. "I know it looks odd to see such a short man in a big vehicle. No, I'm not overcompensating for anything," he said, then winked at her. "I just happen to like big trucks. When I bought this I had it specially customized to fit my stature. The dealership welded blocks on the clutch pedal. They put smaller blocks on the brake pedal. They also raised the floorboard."

"Um, oh, okay," she said. Ellen realized that he must have plenty of money in order to make all of those changes, but she was seriously unimpressed.

When they arrived at the restaurant she'd chosen Ellen looked around to make sure her escape plan was there. Prior to accepting his invitation to dinner she'd asked Jenise and Reggie to accidentally show up at the same restaurant just in case he turned out to be dangerous or worse and she needed to make a quick exit. The two of them were seated near the front, and Jenise winked at her as she and Butterbean walked by on the way to their table. Reggie burst out laughing, and Jenise had to quiet him down to keep the entire restaurant from staring at him.

"Don't worry about that jerk," Butterbean said as they took their seats. "I get laughed at and stared at all the time. It doesn't bother me because I remind myself that I'm twice as tall as them when I'm standing on my wallet." He smiled broadly at her.

Realizing that she needed to make the most of the situation, Ellen tried her best at polite conversation. "So your profile listed Butterbean as your handle. What's your real name?"

"Butterbean Logan is my real name. It was my mother's favorite bean."

Ellen stared at him in disbelief.

"My mother was kind of spacey. She was probably one of the last leftovers from the hippies of the sixties. I loved her dearly, God rest her soul, but she smoked up most of her brain cells long before I or my siblings were born," he explained in a matter-of-fact manner.

As the evening dragged on, Butterbean told Ellen about his brother that everyone called Hal, but his birth name was Jalapeño. Their mother had named him after her favorite pepper. And he couldn't leave out his sister, Holiday, who was not born on Christmas, Easter, or even Arbor Day. She was born during one of the hottest summers on record in Brooklyn, New York. Butterbean explained that at that time his mother was one of those people that you'd see on *Oprah Winfrey* or TLC who said they didn't realize they were pregnant until their water broke. She was standing in front of the street cart that she sold homemade necklaces from wishing for a holiday when she suddenly doubled over in pain. It made perfect sense to her that her daughter should be named Holiday as she is what turned up immediately after her wish.

He also felt no embarrassment in telling her that his mother died in a mysterious accident while visiting his father's family in Alabama. He openly told her that although it was never proved, most people believed that his paternal grandmother had pushed her down a flight of stairs because she couldn't believe that her handsome, educated black son had married such a homely piece of poor white trash.

Later, Butterbean remarked that Ellen had beautiful skin, and she briefly thought that he was giving her an actual compliment. Then he followed it up by stating that he normally did not date black women, but he made an exception in her case due to her light complexion. If things worked out the way he hoped they would, he told her he was sure they wouldn't end up with any tar babies for children.

The date went steadily downhill from that point as she struggled to keep from barfing while watching his atrocious table manners. Butterbean chewed his food with his mouth gaping wide open. The few times that he did close his mouth he smacked his big pink lips so loud the patrons at the next table could overhear the sound. As if he was down home on a farm in Kentucky, he took his bread and sopped up the sauce from his plate, then shoved it toward Ellen to take a bite. Declining, she glanced over at Jenise and Reggie to give them the signal that she was ready to leave, but they were too engrossed in each other to notice.

When it seemed to Ellen that things could not get any worse he decided to explain to her why he did not believe in God. Ellen was flabbergasted as the Web site they'd met on was supposed to be for Christian singles. Butterbean explained that he was not a Christian and he wholeheartedly did not believe that God existed. He felt the notion of someone being able to have three parts, the Father, the Son, and the Holy Ghost, was absolutely ridiculous.

Although something inside her told her that she'd live to regret it, Ellen could not help asking why, if he felt that way, he joined a dating site for Christians. His answer was just the catalyst she needed to get up from the table and walk out on him. Grinning from ear to ear, he calmly stated that regardless of their religious fantasies, Christian girls were always the freakiest in bed. Ellen was surprised that she didn't leave skid marks on the floor as she rushed over to her sister's table and begged them to take her home.

Still laughing as she pulled into the parking lot of Cedric's catering, Ellen could not help but thank God that she had dodged that bullet and subsequently found Semaj, who was the love of her life.

"He's put on weight," Jenise said. "Now the name Butterbean fits him perfectly." Glad to see her sister finally smiling she reached for the car door.

They got out of the car and went inside. As soon as the clerk asked where Semaj was, Jenise noticed the cloud wash over her sister's face again.

"Um, he couldn't make it, but I brought my sister along to help me choose the menu."

Noticing the look on her face the clerk did his best to reassure her. "That's fine. We've done tastings with all of the bridesmaids and both mothers. Wedding planning is usually a female thing. Don't let it bother you, honey."

Ellen appreciated his encouragement, but it wasn't the fact that Semaj was missing the tasting that bothered her most. It was the fact that within a few shorts weeks she'd begun to wonder if the man she was about to marry was who she'd always thought he was.

It began with his mood changing drastically after his four-day disappearance. Then just when she thought things were back on track, they began to spiral out of control again. She'd noticed that he was always on edge and constantly taking phone calls that he didn't want her to overhear. A few of the times she'd noticed that the person on the caller ID was Semaj's cousin, Rip, and that worried her. Even though he claimed to be on the right side of the law since his shooting and subsequent hospital stay, Ellen remembered the Rip that used to rule the projects she grew up in with an iron fist and 9 mm gun. By that time, her parents had moved their family away from the projects and into a nice house in the suburbs, but Ellen had many friends and relatives who still resided there. They gave her information on the downward spiral the neighborhood was taking due to drugs, and she also knew who was responsible. Rip. Although he'd never gotten his own hands dirty, she knew he'd given the order that resulted in the shooting, stabbing, or beating of many of the residents of Sand Poole Manor.

For years, she'd blamed him solely for the demise of her cousin, Gigi. Of course, the police said that Gigi had died from a heart attack in an abandoned apartment that had become a crack house, but Ellen was well aware that it was prolonged use of cocaine that damaged her twenty-three-year-old heart. Even before her death, it pained Ellen and Jenise as they watched the little girl they used to play dolls with grow into a crack zombie, selling her body for one more hit. If it had not been for Rip and others like him, who sold their people's souls for a few dollars, Ellen was sure her cousin would still be alive.

When Semaj had told her during their first month of dating that he wanted her to meet his cousin and best friend, Marion, she had no idea that it was the notorious Rip from Sand Poole Manor. He was almost unrecognizable after the weight loss, but he confirmed during their first meeting that he indeed was the legend. Since that time, Rip had always treated her with respect, and she'd almost begun to actually look at him as a different person. That was, until Semaj began acting erratically every time his phone rang and Rip was on the other end. It also wasn't lost on her that when he'd disappeared and gone home to Andrus, S.C., Rip was the only person who seemed to know about it. In the past, their closeness had not bothered Ellen, but every time she prayed, the Spirit warned her that this was totally different. She knew what Rip was capable of, and it terrified her to think that Semaj now seemed to be his right-hand man.

"Ellen, who is this beautiful model you've brought with you today?" Cedric asked. He walked into the lobby area to greet them.

"This is my sister and matron of honor, Jenise Murphy." She turned to her sister. "Jenise, this is the best chef in all of Atlanta, and my classmate from North Carolina A&T, Cedric Grier."

Jenise extended her hand to Cedric and warmly shook it. "It's a pleasure to meet you, Mr. Grier," she said.

"Call me Cedric, everyone does. Follow me, ladies."

He took them into a room that looked like a private dining room. The round table was set with a white tablecloth and an emerald green lace overlay. In the center of the table was an eighteen inch tall vase filled with green apples, water, and a floating candle on top. The place setting was white plate with gold trim that Ellen and Semaj had chosen as their china setting. Around the table were two chairs with a white covering and an emerald green sash tied around the back. Ellen's mouth fell open, and she gasped with delight when she saw it.

"This is stunning!" Jenise said.

"I know that you only hired me to do the food, Ellen, but this is my vision for your reception décor. What do you think?"

Slowly, Ellen walked over to the table and traced her fingers along the silk tablecloth. Tears welled up in her eyes, and she turned to look at Cedric. "I think it's the most exquisite thing I've ever seen."

Cedric beamed with pride. "Thank you. Now just let me get another chair and an additional plate. Is Semaj on his way?"

Once again Ellen's face fell as she remembered her fiancé and the way he'd been acting for the past couple of weeks. She looked at her sister, and then at Cedric. "Semaj is . . . I mean, he has been . . . I'm sorry you've gone to so much trouble. Everything is beautiful, and I'm sure the food tastes absolutely wonderful."

The tears that had welled up in her eyes earlier began to fall down her cheeks. Cedric thought they were tears of joy, but Jenise knew better. She rushed over and put her arms around her sister. "Sissy, are you okay?"

"Take me home, Jenise," she sobbed. "The wedding is off," she said.

Chapter Ten

Reggie sat in the radio station lobby twiddling his thumbs impatiently as he waited for the receptionist to take him to the back for his appointment. He'd received a phone call from the DJ after he'd watched one of Reggie's videos on YouTube. He sent him a message asking him to stop by with a demo for him to listen to and to discuss the possibility of having Reggie's songs played on the radio. It was a small local radio station, but Reggie realized that Atlanta was a huge town that was home to hundreds of celebrities and even on a small station he could be heard by the right person.

He waited for more than an hour for the receptionist to return. He was beginning to feel discouraged when to his surprise and delight, the owner, Curtis Jansen, who was also the Sunday morning DJ, walked out the door with his hand extended.

"Reggie, it's a pleasure to meet the man behind the music. Your video was great, and I absolutely love the demo that you brought in. Come into my office and let's talk business," he said.

The meeting went fabulously. Curtis told Reggie that he wanted to hear more of his music and he intended to feature him on the following Sunday's morning show. He also told him that he had recently purchased a small studio and was interested in starting his own record label. If he was willing, he wanted Reggie to be his first artist. Curtis believed that with Reggie's talent and the exposure he could give him on the radio station they were both sure to make a lot of money. Although they didn't sign anything, Reggie happily agreed, and Curtis advised that he'd be hearing from his attorney soon to finalize the agreement. An hour later, an elated Reggie rushed into their apartment filled with excitement.

"Jenise, Jenise!" he screamed.

He went into the bedroom, the bathroom, and the kitchen, but he still couldn't find her anywhere. "That heffa ain't never here when I need her," he said to himself. He opened the refrigerator, pulled out a beer, twisted off the cap, turned it up, and reached in for another one to take with him to the living room. He got comfortable on the couch watching basketball and drinking beer while he waited for Jenise to return home.

The sound of Jenise opening the front door awoke him from his drunken stupor. He sat up and turned his wrist to check his watch. "Where you been, girl?" he demanded. "It's almost midnight."

"Shhh, Aaliyah's sleeping," she answered softly. Jenise was carrying her daughter in her arms. She walked past Reggie and took Aaliyah to her bedroom, then laid her down.

Reggie sat on the couch angrily awaiting her return. As soon as she entered the living room he began his tirade. "I asked you where you have been. Don't make me ask again," he sneered.

"I told you earlier that I was going shopping with Ellen."

"You've been gone all day and half the night. Do you think I'm stupid or something? The mall closed a long time ago. Anyway, if you went shopping where are your bags?"

As he continued chastising her like a little girl, his voice got louder and louder and the accusations flew right and left. Even though she had a reasonable explanation for every second of the time that she was gone, she'd learned a long time ago that there was no use in trying to explain that to Reggie. It seemed to her that hearing the truth only made him angrier, and she'd come to the realization that he didn't want the truth; he wanted to be right. If she explained her whereabouts, it would only prove his anger wrong, and the last thing Reggie wanted to be was wrong. Instead of further agitating him with a reasonable explanation, she decided to sit quietly and allow him to continue his rant in the hopes that he'd get tired of hearing himself yell and finally shut up.

Things had not always been so bad between them. Jenise began reminiscing about the good times with Reggie soon after learning her sister was engaged. While Ellen seemed to struggle with finding the right one before meeting Semaj, Jenise met Reggie her freshman year in high school and they'd been together ever since. Their initial meeting happened when they both auditioned for the high school Glee club.

Jenise's earliest memory of singing had been when she was five years old. Her mother often told the story to anyone who would listen. Deloris had been in the kitchen one Saturday evening preparing her Sunday dinner because she wholeheartedly believed in keeping the Sabbath day holy. Each Saturday evening she'd serve her family hot dogs, hamburgers, or some other meal that was easy to prepare; then she'd cook her Sunday dinner and place it in the refrigerator overnight. After the family attended church service on Sunday morning, she'd warm up the dinner in the oven, thereby not committing a sin by working on a Sunday.

That particular evening, Deloris was busy flouring chicken pieces for frying. Malcolm had taken Ellen across town to her weekly piano lesson, and Deloris and Jenise were alone in the apartment when she heard a small, yet strong voice wafting from the bedroom. She wiped her hands on her apron and went down the hallway to the girl's room. Inside, she saw Jenise had lined her collection of Barbie dolls and Teddy bears up as if they were a church choir, and she was their director. Without making a sound, Deloris listened quietly as her five-year-old daughter sang her favorite hymn.

"When I've gone the last mile of the way, I shall rest at the close of the day; And I know there are joys that await me, When I've gone the last mile of the way."

Fighting back tears, Deloris could hardly believe how melodious the tones were. It astounded her that she knew all of the words, but it impressed her even more that Jenise hit each and every note with almost perfect pitch.

The next Saturday morning Jenise became the newest member of The Sunbeam Children's choir at their church. By the time she was ten years old, she was the featured soloist. Everywhere the choir sang people were in awe of the little girl with the big anointed voice. Jenise loved to sing. It made her feel appreciated, and it was the only time that people didn't point out how dark skinned she was. If she had her way, Jenise would have sung every word that she spoke because it was the only time that she believed that it made people look past her chocolate skin and actually see how beautiful she was inside.

By the time she was a freshman in high school, Jenise was a confident and strong soprano when she stepped in front of the judges and auditioned to join the Glee club. She'd stood in churches all over the state of Georgia and brought tears to the eyes of an entire congregation, so there was no doubt in her mind that she possessed the skills to be a member. All of her singing up until that point had been within the confines of her church at her parents' insistence, but she was ready to learn how to sing other songs beside hymns and spirituals. She knew that she possessed a God-given talent, but she also believed that by being a member of the Glee club she would receive the proper training that she believed that she needed in order to nurture that gift.

After her successful audition, Jenise decided to hang around and listen to some of the others who were also auditioning. Several girls squeaked out weak renditions of the latest pop songs. Jenise noticed that most of the guys still sang in a high register as their voices had not begun to change. Reggie Murphy was the last to step out on the stage. Jenise was not initially impressed. She felt that he was fairly cute, but way too skinny. However, when he opened his mouth to sing, she was not only overwhelmed with his lush bravado and perfect pitch, she was mesmerized by him.

The two of them began dating, and they often sang duets together at talent shows, showcases, and churches throughout their home state of Georgia, and they'd even traveled as far away as Virginia and Ohio. They had magic when they sang secular duets, but the anointing that poured down when they sang gospel was indescribable. Jenise loved the passion and power that Reggie had when he sang, and it wasn't long before both of them felt that same passion toward each other.

On her eighteenth birthday, Jenise discovered that she was pregnant. She'd suspected it for several weeks, but honestly believed that if she ignored it, that maybe it would not be true. She confided in her older sister, and Ellen accompanied her to a doctor who advised that she was already three months along. Crying in the car as they drove home, Jenise worried about how in the world she would be able to break the news to her parents. In less than a week she would be graduating from high school, and she'd already received an acceptance letter and a full scholarship from Spelman College's music department. Being devout Christians, she knew that her parents would be sorely disappointed.

Malcolm Winston's demeanor after hearing the news surprised everyone. Ellen suggested that Jenise tell both of her parents following dinner that evening, and she held her sister's hand while she spoke for moral support. They watched their father as Jenise shared her news, prepared to hear him yell, scream, or even cry, but no emotion showed on his face at all. Instead, he calmly walked into the kitchen, picked up the phone that was hanging on the wall, and called Reggie's father.

"May I speak with Reverend Clarence Murphy," he said.

The two men spoke for less than ten minutes. As a result of their intense conversation, Jenise graduated high school, announced her engagement, had a bridal shower, and became Reggie's wife, all within the same month. Although Reggie fought it, his father demanded that he give up his plans to attend Julliard in the fall and do the right thing by Jenise. In exchange, he cosigned for the two of them to move into a nice two-bedroom apartment, bought them new furniture, and hired Reggie as his church's musical director. It didn't pay much, but it allowed him the free time that he needed to work on his other music projects. Jenise was disappointed that she would not be attending Spelman, but she reasoned that she had the rest of her life to go back to school. She'd begun to feel happy and excited as she anticipated becoming a mother.

For about three months the newlyweds led what Jenise believed was a happy life. Jenise took a job working
in a call center for the local telephone company, and
although money was tight she was happy and in love
. . . until the night Reggie came home angry, drank
six beers in less than a half hour, and she discovered
the abusive man that she'd married. Throughout their
courtship he'd never been mean, or sullen, and never
violent, and even with the burning sensation that ran
across her cheek when he slapped her, Jenise could not
believe that he'd actually hit her.

Jenise blamed herself. She knew that Reggie liked to
eat dinner before 7:00 P.M., and she was late cooking
for him that night because she'd gone to the grocery
store after work. He was absolutely right, she reasoned.
If she managed her time better, it never would've happened, and if she made her husband happy, it would
never happen again.

But it did happen again, later that same week. This
time, Reggie was in a rage, and he didn't even need alcohol to fuel it further.

"I am sick of those idiots at my father's church,"
he screamed as he stomped into the apartment and
slammed the door.

"What happened?" Jenise asked. She was flabbergasted at how angry he seemed to be when he returned
from choir rehearsal. Singing God's praises always
made her feel happy and alive, and at one point in their
lives she knew it did the same thing for him. But lately,
it had seemed to have the opposite effect.

"We spent three hours rehearsing the same song,
and they still couldn't get it right. I played their parts
over and over and over again. The tenors couldn't remember it to save their lives. The altos were flat, and
you know the sopranos can't carry a tune without you
there to help them."

By that time, Jenise was almost six months pregnant and after working all day she just couldn't find the energy to go to choir rehearsal. If she'd known how disastrous that one decision would turn out to be, she would have been the first person to arrive.

"I'm sorry, baby. I'll be there next week. I promise," she said.

"Lorrelle tried to sing your solo, and it sounded horrible. I'm sick of dealing with that prima donna. Every note out of her mouth is flatter than ten dimes."

At that point in her marriage Jenise had not learned the art of allowing Reggie to vent without her speaking. In her mind, she believed that if she apologized enough and made enough excuses for the other singers, he would calm down and listen, but she was wrong. While she was trying her best to explain that Lorrelle was recovering from a severe sinus infection that had adversely affected her voice, Reggie looked at her with a fire and rage in his eyes that she'd never seen before in her life. It was as if the fires of Hades had risen up in him and Satan now possessed his entire being. He drew his fist back and punched her with all of his might. Jenise had been standing in front of the couch, but the force of the blow threw her forward into the coffee table. As her stomach smashed against the wood, it shattered into a bunch of pieces and she fell facedown on the floor. Lying in a pool of her own blood she felt a tightening pain in her abdomen and she knew that something was terribly wrong. She waited for Reggie to ask her if she was all right and help her up. However, he merely turned his back to her, walked into their bedroom, and slammed the door.

Crawling across the floor, she managed to reach the phone and dialed 911. When the paramedics rang the doorbell, Reggie finally came out of the bedroom and peered through the peephole.

"Thank God, you finally got here. My wife tripped on the rug and fell onto the coffee table. Please help her," he lied as he let them in.

Jenise knew that she should protest and tell them the truth, but at that moment, her only thought was for the safety of her unborn child. Correcting the paramedics could wait she thought as they turned her over.

"Be careful, she's pregnant," Reggie said. For a moment, Jenise began to believe that he really did care about her and the baby.

To this day, Jenise had never told her family the real truth even though the fall resulted in the miscarriage of her unborn child. Instead, she had accepted Reggie's apology and allowed everyone to believe that it was just an awful accident. She'd also lost two other pregnancies as a result of savage beatings from him. Not even Reggie had been aware of her condition, and she vowed never to breathe a word of it. When she became pregnant with Aaliyah, she knew that she had to do everything in her power to protect her baby. Reggie still hit her at least once a month, but she made sure to always protect her stomach and take the blows to her face. Unfortunately, the consequences of that strategy meant that first Ellen, and then her parents, soon discovered the abuse as she could not hide the black eyes, busted lips, or swollen cheeks. They begged and pleaded with her to leave, but Jenise refused.

That same year, Reggie's father had passed away from colon cancer and another minister had taken over at his church. Not only did Reggie lose his job as musical director, but Jenise had also lost the one person who actually seemed to be able to reason with her husband. Reggie refused to take what he deemed to be a lowly regular job, and instead, concentrated solely on his music, while Jenise struggled to make ends meet.

As a result, they'd had to move out of the apartment his father had leased for them and move to the projects at Sand Poole Manor.

As Jenise held her sister in her arms that afternoon while she sobbed in the middle of the caterer's dining room, she reasoned that no relationship was perfect. Everyone had their problems and with God's love and a lot of prayer, she believed that she could work through the problems in her marriage.

Reggie continued to rant and rave, and she retreated to her secret place as she recited Psalm 91:1–2 from the New Living Translation over and over in her head trying to drown him out. "Those who live in the shelter of the Most High will find rest in the shadow of the Almighty. This I declare about the Lord: He alone is my refuge, my place of safety; he is my God, and I trust him."

Reggie quickly grew tired of ranting and was even more enraged by Jenise obviously ignoring him. He slapped her violently across her face with his open palm several times.

Jenise heard a bloodcurdling scream as she crumpled onto the floor, but she knew it had not come from her.

"Mommy, Mommy are you all right?" Aaliyah cried.

Chapter Eleven

All of Hollywood, the city of Atlanta, and even the entire country had been enthralled by the story of the sudden and unlikely disappearance of Wayne James. He was one of the most beloved and respected men in the entertainment industry. He'd won three Emmy awards for best actor and another two Emmys for best writer for his television show. During his summer hiatus from his show, he'd appeared on Broadway and received a Tony nomination for best actor. He'd also produced, directed, and starred in three movies. He was an author, entertainer, entrepreneur, and philanthropist. In his small hometown of Lawrenceville, N.C., there was an elementary and high school as well as a bridge and a highway that bore the name of their most successful resident. Prior to becoming an actor, he'd attended college and received his bachelor's degree and while filming his successful sitcom, he'd earned a master's and a doctorate degree from UCLA that wasn't honorary. Even with his busy career, he'd taken the classes, written the papers, and actually earned his degree in psychology. He was father to five boys that he'd adopted and raised as his own. Unlike those celebrities who adopted children from foreign nations, Wayne got each of his sons from adoption agencies within the United States as he felt it was his duty to take care of those at home first. He was well respected and loved by his peers and especially his fans. For that reason, no one could understand or fathom the reason that he'd been abducted.

Immediately following his abduction, the police waited with bated breath to receive a letter or phone call from the kidnappers with ransom demands, but none came. He'd been missing for over a week, and the police had only one clue. A fourteen-year-old boy who'd been walking his dog through the condo complex on the evening Wayne went missing had noticed a strange white utility van in the area. It caught his attention because he'd never seen it in the area before or since. He'd first noticed it when he came outside with his dog, and it almost ran over him as it sped out of the parking lot a few moments later.

The police had not been able to locate the van or its driver and without the motive of ransom, many were beginning to lose hope that Wayne would be found alive.

The gossip magazines, tabloid newspapers, and scandalous Web sites were going hog wild with any and every fake story they could find. The *National Enquirer* had bought a photograph that they claimed was taken the night of the abduction that showed Wayne being taken away by a group of terrorists. A fake terrorist group had even taken credit for the abduction. Police analysis soon proved that it had been photo shopped by someone seeking to exploit the crime for profit.

The Web site GMZ ran a story told to them by a person who professed to be an unknown insider that had proof that Wayne had been abducted by aliens from outer space. The insider claimed that Wayne's success was due to a vow he'd made with the aliens to extract mind control over human beings and thus guarantee his spot as a rich and powerful celebrity. However, Wayne had double-crossed the aliens, and they'd come back and snatched him to repay the debt.

One of the rumors running through the projects of Sand Poole Manor and heavily circulated by Gwen was that Wayne had gone into hiding because of personal reasons. Although she had not spoken with him since their lunch at Justin's restaurant, she believed that he had been deeply affected by bringing up the memories of his past. Therefore, she reasoned that he needed some time away from the spotlight, and he'd simply flown to an island somewhere to relax. She was not the least bit consumed with the other rumors and truly believed that he'd be back soon.

"Are you out of your mind?" Rip asked Semaj.

The two of them were standing in the living room of Semaj's apartment, and he'd just informed him that he was scheduled to be a featured guest on Kandyss Kline's talk show. Distraught over her missing friend, Wayne James, Kandyss had decided to dedicate an entire hour of her show to the story. She'd invited several celebrity guests to appear and sing tribute songs. She'd also invited the special police investigator who was in charge of the search to be a guest in the hopes that a viewer would be able to assist in the investigation. Wayne's sons were also scheduled to appear to make an impassioned plea for their father's safe return. Lastly, she'd invited Semaj Matthews, the man whom the city of Atlanta depended on to help find missing persons. He'd been instrumental in reuniting dozens of families with their missing loved ones, and Kandyss felt he was the perfect person to find Wayne.

"No, I'm not out of my mind," he responded. "I couldn't say no to her. I've never turned down anyone who asked me to find their loved one. How could I refuse?"

"You open your mouth, and you say no. This is the definition of conflict of interests. Tell her that you are too busy because you're in the middle of planning your wedding, and you just can't do it."

Semaj sighed and stared at the floor. "Ellen called the wedding off," he whispered.

"What? When did this happen?"

"She told me a few days ago that she was having doubts and that she just couldn't go through with it. I don't know for sure, but I think she was hoping I'd reassure her, but I just couldn't do it. My mind is in a whole other place right now."

Rip swung his fist at the air in frustration. "This is all my fault, man. That girl is your queen. She's your soul mate. I can't believe I messed it up by kidnapping that jerk."

"Don't blame yourself. You may have put the train in motion, but I've been the engineer for the past week. Ellen didn't believe in me anymore since I've messed up my life so terribly."

"What are you talking about? Your life was fine until I screwed up and got you involved in my crime. That's the last straw. I'm going to leave the door unlocked and make sure Wayne can find his way out of the warehouse tonight."

Semaj grabbed Rip by his arm as he turned to walk away. "No, you are not going to do any such thing. I suffered through the loneliness that man caused me for thirty-six years. It certainly won't kill him if he has to feel that way for a few days."

Remorse consumed Rip as he stared at his cousin, not recognizing the man that he'd become. As long as he could remember, he and Semaj had been like peanut butter and jelly. Rip considered himself to be peanut butter. He was dark. Depending on his mood he could be smooth or crunchy, and he always seemed to find himself in a sticky situation. Semaj was just like jelly.

No matter the flavor, the day, or the time, he was always delicious and sweet.

Throughout their lives if there was a choice to be made, Rip always chose to do the wrong thing, while Semaj never hesitated to do the right thing. In school, Semaj made As and Bs while Rip struggled to keep a C average. At the home he shared with his aunt, Rip's bedroom was a pullout couch in the living room with flat pillows. Since he had little privacy he rarely bothered to tidy it up. In contrast, Semaj had a large bedroom with bunk beds that his grandparents had put in so that he could invite Rip over to stay whenever he wanted. On lazy Saturday mornings when Rip wanted to head down to the creek and go fishing or fly kites in the field behind their house, Semaj, who was the responsible one, wouldn't leave until he'd cleaned his room and completed all of the chores that his grandmother assigned him. After that, he'd put in at least an hour helping his grandfather out at the barbershop and only then would he agree to goof off and be a regular kid with Rip. His goody-two-shoes behavior did not bother Rip at all. In fact, he greatly admired it. He'd often wished that he could be more like Semaj, but also felt that the cards had been dealt differently for him.

The two of them shared a bond in that neither grew up with a father in their home. Rip always envied Semaj, however, because while Rip was raised by his aunt with no male role models to look up to, Semaj had the benefit of his grandfather who was a wonderful man and a pillar of the community.

Alvin Matthews was known as Pop Al to everyone in Andrus. He was the owner and proprietor of the local barbershop after having earned his barber's license while in the army. His barbershop had four chairs, and all of the other barbers paid rent directly to him.

Beginning when he was ten years old up until he was seventeen, Pop Al gave Semaj a job at the barbershop sweeping up hair after school and on Saturdays. While he cut hair and Semaj swept, he gave his grandson the benefit of his years of wisdom. Pop Al taught Semaj the value of hard work, the importance of an education, and how to treat girls and women with respect. Most importantly, he taught him to always read his Bible, trust in God, and to pray.

The first week that he was in the juvenile detention home after stealing from the store, Rip received a visit from Semaj and Pop Al. Even though they all knew Rip's actions were wrong, Pop Al taught Semaj not to turn his back on his friends, and more significantly, his family. He received regular visits from the two of them up until Pop Al passed away.

During his junior year in high school, when he was sixteen, Pop Al taught Semaj how to drive and helped him to obtain his driver's license. That summer, he presented Semaj with his first car. It was an old, used Chevy with no backseat, but it set Semaj apart from his peers as he was one of only a few teens in their small town that had their own car.

The only contact Rip had with his father was through letters he sent him weekly from the state prison. In Rip's opinion, he couldn't teach him how to be a man because he didn't know himself. He'd met Rip's mother while stationed in Japan as a member of the air force. They eloped three weeks after meeting and returned to the States. Rip was born at Elgin Air Force Base in Florida and before he was a year old his father had been transferred to Lakeland Air Force Base in San Antonio, Texas. He came home drunk one night and noticed Rip's mother on the phone speaking in Japanese. Believing she was doing so in order to hide a relationship with an-

other man, he overreacted, took out his pistol, and shot
her twice in the face. During his trial, he broke down and
cried when it was revealed that the man on the other end
of the phone was her grandfather who did not speak any
English. He received a life sentence without the possibility of parole.

His weekly letters to Rip were filled with remorse
and regret, and Rip truly appreciated the effort. Yet no
matter what, he could not and would not ever forgive
him for taking his mother's life. Rip was living in Sand
Poole Manor at the height of his drug game when he received word that his father had been stabbed and killed
in prison by another inmate. In order to prevent him
from being buried in a field reserved for prisoners with
no family, Rip paid for his body to be cremated and
shipped to Atlanta. He didn't bother with a funeral or
even a memorial service. Instead, Rip had him buried
in a local cemetery and paid for a modest headstone.
Every Father's Day, he stopped by and left a single red
rose.

Once during a visit from Semaj and Pop Al to the
detention facility, Rip wanted to show his appreciation
for their regular visits. Although the guards sometimes
ate the majority of the contents, he also appreciated
the cookies that Semaj's grandmother Nettie sent him
every month. While sitting in the visitors' lounge and
munching on a chocolate chip, Rip remarked to Semaj
that he thought Pop Al was the best father any boy
could ever have.

"He's not my father. He's my *grand*father," Semaj
corrected him.

Pop Al's face washed over with a sudden sadness,
and Rip could tell that he was hurt by the comment.
He'd treated Semaj like his own son for his entire life,
and Rip could not believe he wasn't eternally grate-

ful. Rip was sitting in a detention home and had no mother, an incarcerated father, and only a poor aunt to call family. Semaj had his wonderful grandparents, a room of his own, a closet full of clothes that included the latest Jordan sneakers and jeans that were actually still in style. He had a car, he had money that his grandparents put into his pocket, and in Rip's opinion, he had a great life.

Still feeling Semaj's tight grip on his arm, Rip realized that he didn't understand it then, and he certainly didn't understand it now. Standing before him was a man with a truly successful life. He had a great career in journalism. He owned his condo as well as the property his grandparents had left him when they passed away. He had a beautiful, smart fiancée who loved him dearly. Even with all of that, Rip knew that Semaj was still missing something. It wasn't material, and it wasn't physical, but emotionally, he was missing something that only a father could provide.

"All right, I won't let him out, but we can't hold the man indefinitely," he said. He pulled his arm from Semaj's grasp.

"I don't plan to. I should have the DNA results back by tomorrow."

Earlier that week, Semaj had asked Rip to find a way to get a swab of Wayne James in order to do a DNA test. The task had been fairly easy. Since he'd been held captive Rip returned to the warehouse each night and gave Wayne food and water. In order to protect his identity, he always went under the cover of darkness, and he never let Wayne see his face. That particular evening he told Wayne to open his mouth. Wayne complied, believing that Rip was about to pour water into it as he'd done the previous nights. Instead, he stuck the swab in and collected a DNA sample. He took the sample to Semaj, and he'd mailed it off for the results. In order to rush things along, he'd paid for overnight shipping, but he'd received an e-mail advising him that there was a delay due to a backlog and the results were due to arrive the next day.

Although every fiber of his being told him that Wayne James was his father, he couldn't shake the feeling that maybe he was wrong. Doubt had crept in, and he began to wonder why Wayne had so adamantly denied it during their meeting. He also wondered why Wayne had told Gwen that his son died in that fire so he'd tried to find the newspaper article that she claimed to have seen. Because it had been so many years before he couldn't find anything listed on the Internet. He'd considered flying to Chicago to check the microfilm office of the newspaper, but he couldn't get away from work and he really wanted to be a part of the show being done by Kandyss Kline. The DNA results would be definitive proof, but Semaj also wanted a chance to obtain access to everything the police had regarding Wayne's disappearance. He wanted to meet Wayne's adopted sons and hear about the real father that they knew at home. Everything in him needed to hear them talk about the father they loved that he'd been denied.

"So what if things go as planned and your package shows up as scheduled tomorrow?" Rip asked. "What are you planning to do after you get the DNA results?"

"I'm going confront him with the undeniable truth. When we started this whole thing, you said you were trying to grant me my wish of being able to talk to him and get some answers. Well, that's exactly what I intend to do."

Rip nodded his head. "Then you don't need to go on this stupid talk show. DNA is all that you need to confront him with."

"I told you already that there was no way that I could refuse. Finding people who are missing is what I do best. I've found people who'd been missing for as long as ten years. The city of Atlanta has too much faith in me. I can't let them down."

A sarcastic laugh came out of Rip's mouth. "You won't let the city of Atlanta down, but you have no problem with letting Ellen down?"

Semaj shot him an angry glare, and then began pacing back and forth across the room. "Ellen was tripping. She told me that she saw me that day with Gwen, when we were on our way to meet Wayne. Then she accused me of having an affair with her. I have never cheated on Ellen, and I never would. Then when I told her that Gwen was your friend and that I was just giving her a ride to help you out, she said that I was using you to cover up my indiscretions. Can you believe that?"

Rip nodded. "Actually, I can. Think about it. You've been lying to her since the first meeting you had with Gwen. You didn't tell her about meeting Wayne. Then you went to Andrus without so much as a phone call to let her know. She deserves better than that."

"Her sister has a man who blacks her eye on a regular basis, so Ellen should be thankful to have a man who treats her with respect. I admit I've been moody and a little distant, but that's not enough to throw away our relationship over. I'm not a cheater, and she'd know that if she truly knew me."

Noticing how agitated Semaj was becoming as he continued to pace back and forth, Rip slowly shook his head. He totally understood why Ellen might think she didn't know Semaj anymore, because he was beginning to feel exactly the same way. The key to Semaj's turmoil was locked inside a warehouse where Rip had hidden him. His method left a lot to be desired but Rip realized that getting Semaj together with his father was the only thing that would quench the fire of hurt and betrayal that was burning in his spirit.

"So what do you want me to do while you're on TV pretending to help find Wayne James?" Rip asked. He took a seat on the couch and crossed his legs.

Semaj finally stopped pacing and turned to face his cousin. A wide wicked grin covered his face. "That's the beauty of my entire plan. I will appear on the show, get all the clues that police have, and then I'm going to be the one to find Wayne James."

"What do you mean *find* him? We already know where he is. Besides, how can you be the one to find him and the one who confronts him? You're not making sense."

Rip knew how to cover his tracks impeccably, and he had no fear of being found out by the police or even the FBI. Compared to his days as a drug kingpin running a million dollar a week business from the comfort of his apartment, kidnapping was a snap. On the night he'd taken Wayne, he'd worn black jeans, a black sweater, black gloves, and a black ski mask. He wasn't sure if the condo had security cameras or not, so he used a disguise that he knew would hide his identity. He'd switched out the license plates on the utility van, just in case anyone noticed it driving away from the scene. When he returned it to the associate that he'd borrowed it from, Rip told him that he'd had a minor accident and damaged the right side. Instead of bringing him back a banged up van, he'd had it painted blue at his own expense. His associate was thankful and totally unaware of the real reason his van had been altered. Now that Semaj was involved, Rip had begun to worry about him making mistakes and being sloppy.

"After I get the DNA results with my proof, then I am going to stumble upon the warehouse, find Wayne James, and release him. I'll be a national hero. The fans and the media will love me. Most important, Wayne James will owe me a debt of gratitude. He'll say to me, 'Mr. Matthews, is there anything that I can do for you? I owe you my life,' then I'll say, 'You can admit to me and the world that you are my biological father.'" Semaj began pacing again and rubbed his hands together in anticipation. "Oh, he'll deny it again. I'm sure of it, but I will have my proof. If that isn't enough, I'll schedule us as guests on *The Maury Show*. Then the whole world will be watching when Maury tells him, 'Wayne James, you *are* the father.'"

Rip rubbed his chin and thought for a moment. Semaj's plan was actually better than his. He'd planned to release Wayne on a secluded road with a hood over his head so that he wouldn't remember where he'd been held captive. That was going to be after Semaj had the opportunity to talk to him, man to man, face to face. In his mind, the entire situation should not have taken more than twenty-four hours, and he believed that if Wayne James had any integrity, he would not try to press charges against Semaj.

All of that changed when Semaj decided to become involved and insisted that they allow Wayne to sit alone in the dark for a few days to replicate the way he'd felt as a child without him. Then Semaj decided that he wanted to do the DNA test and what should have ended within a few hours had elapsed into well over a week's time that the two of them had held a man captive. There was no way that Wayne would not press charges at this point if he had any idea that Semaj or Rip was involved. His only issue with the plan was that Semaj seemed to have lost focus of his original goal. Rip's goal was avenge the way Wayne had treated

Semaj. That was his way of doing things. He was peanut butter and in this situation, he was being crunchy.
But he'd expected his partner jelly to bring him back to
the right side of the bread by convincing him that all he
wanted was a conversation with his father. He didn't
wish him any harm. He didn't want to embarrass him.
He just wanted to talk and as always, do things the
right way. In the end, Rip believed that Semaj would
ensure that everything would turn out sweet. That was
not happening, so he looked up at his cousin and ex-
pressed his concern.

"Revenge is not your style, Semaj. How do you expect to have a real relationship with your father if you
begin it by forcing him to owe you a debt of gratitude?
Then your next move is public embarrassment. This
isn't like you, man."

Semaj suddenly swung his leg out and kicked over
the coffee table. Rip sat in stunned silence, shocked at
how he was unexpectedly acting. Semaj walked over
to Rip and stood over him, bellowing at the top of his
lungs.

"I stood by your black behind when you got arrested
at fourteen and went to jail. I came to visit you every
day when you were lying in a hospital bed fighting for
your life after DEA agents pumped you full of bullets. I
hired you an attorney with my own money, and I never
asked for a penny of it back. I've been your friend, your
confidant, and your defender your entire life, and now
when I ask you to help me with one thing, you want to
give me lip? Get this and get it good. I'm driving this
car. Get in or get run over. I'm tired of you, Ellen, and
everyone else trying to tell me what's not like me. You
don't know me! You don't know who I really am!" he
seethed.

Semaj stormed down the hallway and slammed his
bedroom door before Rip could respond.

Chapter Twelve

Ellen sat at her desk staring into space. Ever since she'd called off her engagement she just couldn't concentrate on anything work related. As the office manager for a real estate office, she had a large stack of lease agreements that she needed to fax to the home office. The days she'd already taken off to run errands for the wedding had taken its toll on her workload. Ellen was way behind and still unable to focus on her duties enough to be productive. Even though she'd told Semaj that she couldn't marry him she still could not bring herself to tell her parents, her friends, or even her pastor. In her despair, she had not taken the time to call the bakery, the printer, or the florist to cancel her orders. Other than Semaj, no one knew except her sister and Cedric. After her meltdown, they'd both told her to take some time and think about her feelings before making a final decision. Ellen had tried to do just that, and after pulling herself together, she'd called Semaj to discuss their relationship. What began as a quiet, civil talk soon escalated into a full-scale screaming match filled with accusations, denials, and regret. When all was said and done, she'd called off the wedding and hung up on Semaj.

For the life of her, Ellen could not understand the abrupt change in his behavior. She accused him of cheating, but she just threw it out in desperation. She really did not believe that at all. Then she insinuated that Rip was covering for and protecting him. Semaj vehemently denied it. That theory didn't make much sense to her either, but she was grasping at straws in

an attempt to get Semaj to open up and tell her what
was truly going on. The two of them had never had a
problem with communication, and Ellen believed that
Semaj had shared with her his deepest secrets and feelings. She'd often remarked to her friends and cowork-
ers that Semaj wasn't just Mr. Right, he was also Mr.
Do Right. Ellen sincerely believed, beyond a shadow of
a doubt, that he'd always do what was right.

However, she no longer felt that way as she'd witnessed him do a lot of wrong in a few short weeks. While
he may not have been having an affair with Gwen, Ellen knew for sure that he'd lied to her about knowing
her and spending time with her. The man that she once
could set her watch by had missed appointments, ignored phone calls, and totally dropped out of sight for
days. Worst of all, the calm demeanor that she'd grown
to love, no matter the crisis, had dissipated into thin air.
Semaj was edgy, irritable, and downright mean to her.
During the entire time that she'd known him, Ellen had
rarely heard him raise his voice, yet he'd snapped at and
yelled at her several times in the past week. His anger
reminded her of Reggie, and that was a comparison she
hated to make. She loved him dearly, but there was no
way she could go into a marriage under the current circumstances.

Unable to concentrate, Ellen decided to just go home
and began making phone calls to put the final nail in
the coffin of what had previously been her wedding.
She entered her apartment and went into her bedroom
to change out of her blue power suit that she'd worn
to work. In her bedroom, she changed into a pair of
leggings and a big roomy T-shirt. She returned to the
living room, plopped down on her sofa, grabbed her
wedding notebook, took a deep breath, then picked up
her phone. Before she could dial the first phone number there was a knock at her front door.

"IPS delivery," the man on the other side answered after Ellen asked who was there.

She opened the door and signed for the package. As soon as she closed the door, tears began to stream down her face. Although she had not opened the package yet, Ellen realized that it was her wedding gown.

At the beginning of her engagement, Ellen had made the traditional trip to a bridal salon to try on dresses. She'd taken Jenise, her mother Deloris, and her two sorority sisters, Melanie and Latisha, who were also her bridesmaids.

The ladies arrived at the salon and were greeted by an overly chipper attendant named Misty who led them to a private area that had a couch for the ladies to sit. The sofa was facing a large area with mirrors that led to a dressing room. Misty asked Ellen to give her an idea about what type of dress she was looking for, then she brought out several choices for her to try on.

"That doesn't flatter your figure at all," Deloris said when Ellen walked out in the first dress. It was a heavy ball gown with tons of sequins. Ellen felt as if she was dragging an albatross around, and she completely agreed with her mother's opinion.

"Girl, no," Melanie exclaimed as soon as she turned around in dress number two. "That looks like the same dress Peaches got married in last year. She is not someone that you want to imitate, trust."

A parade of four more dresses continued, and no one liked anything that Ellen tried on, including Ellen. Each dress had something about it that she loved, while at the same time, having something about it that she hated. The entire afternoon was beginning to resemble a bad episode of *Say Yes to the Dress,* and Ellen was growing weary and discouraged.

"We have hundreds of dresses, and I'm here to help you," Misty said. "I'm going to bring out a few more choices."

"No, I can't take anymore," Ellen exclaimed.

"Don't give up so soon, Sissy," Jenise said. "When you see your dream dress, you'll know it."

Ellen sighed and joined her sister on the couch. "I'm not giving up at all. I just don't think I'm going to find the perfect dress today."

"A lot of brides need more than one visit before they can make a decision. Would you like for me to schedule you a new appointment?"

Ellen agreed to come back at another time, but she never did. On the advice of a coworker she decided to look for her wedding dress online. Her sister's words had been prophetic because the moment Ellen saw the dress, she intuitively knew it was the right one. The Web site had great reviews so Ellen took a gamble and ordered her dress from a factory in China.

Hoping the dressmaker had made a horrific error that would make her glad she had to send the dress back, Ellen ripped open the package and pulled it out. Now, sitting in her living room, she bawled openly with the most gorgeous wedding dress she'd ever seen in her entire life sitting in her lap. Her crying was so loud that she barely heard another knock at her front door. Quickly wiping her tears with the back of her hands, Ellen went to answer it.

"Who's there?" she called out.

"It's your mother," Deloris answered.

Ellen tried her best to hide the evidence of her tears; then she opened the door and smiled at her mother.

"What are you doing here, Mommy?" she asked. She pulled her into a warm hug and invited her into the apartment.

Deloris walked inside and immediately noticed the wedding dress sprawled out on the sofa. "Well, I went by your office to invite you to lunch, and they said you'd gone home sick. So I came by to check on you. I see your wedding dress has arrived. Did you try it on yet?" she asked excitedly.

Ellen shook her head no and fought back more tears.

"What's wrong, Ellen? Don't say that it's nothing because I've known something was bothering you since the day I picked up Aaliyah from the mall. Tell me what's going on."

Ellen sat down on the couch and began blubbering again. "I called off my wedding. Semaj has changed. It's like I don't know him anymore. He's become secretive, sullen, and mean. He's lied to me and often ignores my phone calls. We had a big fight, and I told him that I couldn't marry him," she whimpered.

Deloris pulled her daughter into her arms and gently rubbed her back as she cried. Without saying a word she allowed Ellen to get it all out. When she thought she was ready to listen she finally spoke.

"What did Semaj say when you called off the wedding?"

"Nothing. I hung up on him after I said it. He didn't even call me back to try to talk me out of it. He just let me go without even putting up a fight."

Deloris took Ellen's face into her hands and looked her straight in the eyes. "Do you love Semaj?"

Ellen sniffed loudly. "Of course I do, but . . ."

"No buts, that's all I needed to know. Where's your Bible?"

Confused, Ellen pointed in the direction of her bedroom. "It's on the nightstand by my bed."

"I'll be right back." Deloris went into Ellen's bedroom and came back carrying her New Living Translation Bible. She flipped through the pages one by one, then finally stopped at a scripture. "Read this," she instructed.

Ellen obediently took the Bible from her mother and began to read aloud. "Love is patient and kind. Love is not jealous or boastful or proud or rude. It does not demand its own way. It is not irritable, and it keeps no record of being wronged. It does not rejoice about injustice but rejoices whenever the truth wins out. Love never gives up, never loses faith, is always hopeful, and endures through every circumstance.

"Prophecy and speaking in unknown languages and special knowledge will become useless. But love will last forever!"

She glanced up at her mother, and then remembered her Bible school training. "Thus, I have read 1 Corinthians 13:4–8. May the Lord add a blessing to the readers and doers of his Word."

"Now tell me, have you been patient and kind with Semaj?"

Feeling shamed Ellen shook her head no.

"Have you been jealous, bragging, or arrogant?"

Ellen nodded to indicate yes and wiped away a tear.

"I don't think I need to go any further. You understand what I'm getting at. You say that you love the man, but you also admit that you haven't been acting like it."

Closing the Bible and placing it back on the table, Ellen turned to her mother to protest. "Neither has he, Mom. He hasn't acted like he loves me in several weeks."

"You are not responsible for the way that Semaj acts. You are only responsible for the way that you act. Now if you could honestly say to me that you'd been acting like the strong Christian woman that I raised you to be, and he was acting a complete fool, then I'd applaud your decision to call off your wedding. But we both know that's not the truth, is it?"

"No, ma'am," she answered.

"Now dry up those tears, girl. Both you and Semaj are under a lot of pressure and stress with this upcoming wedding. I don't know everything he's said or done, but I believe that it all has a logical explanation. Be patient; give him some time. How are you going to have a long happy marriage if you give up after your first fight?"

Ellen grabbed a tissue from the box on the end table and blew her nose. "I guess you're right, Mom. I didn't even think about the pressure he must be under. He's been swamped at work covering the disappearance of Wayne James in addition to his anchoring duties. I'm going to give him a call."

"You don't have to call him today. First, you need to meditate on this scripture and pray about the entire situation. Then when you've got a clear head, give him a call, and I bet everything will be fine. Besides, I've been living on nothing but Slim Fast and grilled chicken for two months to fit into my dress, so *somebody* is getting married." Deloris laughed loudly, and then nudged Ellen until she laughed also.

Shortly after her mother left, Ellen gently picked up her wedding gown, placed it on a padded hanger, and carefully put it inside the custom garment bag she'd purchased. Then she hung it up in the back of her bedroom closet.

In order to relax and meditate on the scriptures her mother had given her, Ellen decided to draw herself a hot bath. She undressed, and then lowered her body into the tub to soak. As she lay there relaxing and praying, the Spirit led her back to her first date with Semaj.

Initially she was hesitant to go out with a news reporter. Watching the news each week, she'd developed a serious mistrust of all people in the media. While she was sure the majority of the stories they reported were true, Ellen also believed that much of what they reported was slanted in favor of the reporter's views. It wasn't until she found out about Semaj's work with missing and exploited children and adults that she decided to give him a whirl.

The disaster with Butterbean, as well as a string of bad dates after that had soured her on allowing men to come to her apartment. So instead, she asked Semaj to meet her at the restaurant. That way, if things went badly, she would have her own car to escape in. Also as usual, she'd had someone meet her there as her backup plan. This time, she'd asked Melanie and Latisha to take a seat at the bar and observe. Ellen knew that her sorority sisters would not hesitate to walk right up to the table and rudely end the date if needed.

However, she should not have bothered. The date was amazing. The two of them found that they had many things that made them total opposites. While Ellen loved gospel music, jazz, and R&B soul, Semaj admitted to being a big fan of Christian rap, but Jay-Z was his favorite artist.

They both loved movies, but Ellen like horror and suspense films, while Semaj preferred comedies and action flicks. Even with those differences, they each felt that the other was the yin to their yang. Regardless of their taste in movies, books, and music, they shared the core values that mattered most. They were both Christians who believed that their faith in God and love for their families was more important than any material possession. They loved kids and both dreamed of being parents one day. Ellen felt safe in his presence, and something inside her told her that Semaj would not only be good to her, he'd also be good for her.

During dinner, he'd shared with her that his mother had died tragically while he was an infant, and he'd been raised by his grandparents. They were kind and loving people, and he'd had a wonderful childhood. He also shared that during the spring of his senior year in high school, both of his grandparents had been killed together in a terrible traffic accident caused by a truck driver who'd put in too many hours and fallen asleep at the wheel. As sad as it made him, Semaj told her that he realized it was for the best, as neither of them would have wanted to go on living without the other. Their love was an eternal one, and he hoped to be able to find the same kind of love some day. Ellen was so captivated by Semaj that she found herself swooning at the sound of his voice. Just in case her judgment was clouded by the number of horrible dates she'd had, she decided to excuse herself from the table to speak with her girls at the bar and get their opinion.

"That brotha is fine as frog's hair," Latisha said. "If you don't want him, pass him my way." She gulped down the last of her virgin strawberry margarita and signaled the bartender to bring her another one.

Good looks did not often impress her, but Ellen had to admit that Semaj was very attractive. His skin was light, although not as light as hers, and he had a very low, sexy, faded haircut that reminded her of Shemar Moore. He was almost six foot tall, and he had a slim but muscular build. When he smiled, his teeth were perfect and white behind full lips that she imagined were very soft. She had to admit, he was incredibly sexy.

"Of course he's good looking. He works in television on the news," she said. "The date is going so well. I just was feeling a little unsure of myself."

"Get over it and get back over there," Melanie said. "You've been praying for a good man for a long time, Ellen. I think Semaj is the answer to your prayers."

Ellen had to agree with her. Semaj seemed to be the answer to all of her prayers.

From that night up until a few weeks prior, Ellen had never doubted that he was sent from God. Throughout their relationship, he had treated her with kindness and respect. Every Valentine's Day, she received a bouquet of a dozen red roses, a cute and cuddly teddy bear, and a heart-shaped box of chocolates. Since they'd met, she'd celebrated her birthday three times and Semaj had made each one special. Once, he'd even baked her favorite chocolate caramel cake from scratch. He'd told her it was his grandmother's recipe, but he wanted to do something special for her that no other man had ever done. They'd attended church service, revivals, and Bible Study together, and she knew that he was a man after God's own heart. During their three-year courtship, he had never pressured her to have sex, and their love was pure and chaste. His track record with finding missing persons made him a local hero that was admired by everyone that knew him, and even those who didn't. Some people who are successful talk about all the haters that they have in their lives, but as far as Ellen knew, there was not a soul who hated Semaj.

Lounging in her bathtub, she remembered all of that and suddenly realized that she'd overreacted to his current moods and made a terrible mistake.

She jumped out of the tub and dried off quickly, then put on her pink terry cloth robe. She sat on the edge of her bed and dialed Semaj's number. As she waited for him to answer she tried to recite her apology in her head. After several rings she began to think that once again he was ignoring her phone calls, then someone picked up.

"Hello," a woman said.

"Who is this?" Ellen asked.

"This is Gwen, who is this?"

Ellen hung up the phone without answering the question.

Chapter Thirteen

Jenise stood outside the door of the meeting hall trying to find the courage to walk in to her first support group for women who are victims of domestic violence. It had taken her years to get there, but she knew that it was the right thing for her, Reggie, and especially Aaliyah.

When her daughter walked in on Reggie hitting her, and then subsequently knocking her to the ground, there was no way that Jenise could make an excuse for it. She was lying on the floor stunned from the force of the blows as Aaliyah stood over her crying her little eyes out. In the past, whenever Reggie hit her, Jenise had been able to successfully hide her bruises from her daughter or tell her a fib to satisfy her questions. This time, there was no lie she could tell. Aaliyah had witnessed everything.

"Mommy, are you okay? Mommy, get up," Aaliyah cried.

Trying as hard as she could, Jenise attempted to get up off of the floor and comfort her child.

"Aaliyah, get back in your room!" Reggie screamed.

"No, Mommy's hurt," she answered. Aaliyah reached for the phone. "I'm calling Auntie Ellen," she said.

Reggie wasn't about to let that happen, and he charged at his daughter, knocking the phone out of her hand. "I said, get back in your room!" he screamed even louder.

Aaliyah screamed loudly in fear and turned around and began running down the hall. Reggie knew there was another phone in the bedroom, and he ran after Aaliyah and snatched her up by her waist.

Still lying on the floor, Jenise could not see what was happening, but she heard her daughter screaming wildly.

"Let me go, Daddy. Let me go!" Aaliyah screamed.

A strength she didn't know she had surged through Jenise's body, and she got up off the living-room floor, ran into the kitchen, and grabbed the largest knife she could find. Then she followed the sound of Aaliyah's screams down the hallway. As she walked into Aaliyah's bedroom, she saw Reggie slap her violently across her tiny brown face.

"Leave her alone!" Jenise screamed.

Reggie turned toward the door and saw the blade of the knife pointed right at him. "What do you think you are going to do with that?" he asked.

"Get out of here now, or I will mess you up so bad, only Jesus will be able to save you," Jenise threatened.

"Are you out of your freaking mind?" Reggie yelled.

Jenise didn't know if she was out of her mind or not. All she knew was that he was hitting her daughter, and there was no way she would allow it. He'd hit her more times than she could remember over the years, and she'd taken it. He'd never laid a hand on Aaliyah. However, after seeing him slap her daughter across the face, the proverbial straw had broken the camel's back, and Ellen was done taking abuse from Reggie.

"No, for the first time in years, I've found my right mind. Get out, Reggie, and don't you ever come back!" she shouted.

He stared at her for a few seconds until he realized that she was deadly serious.

"You are gonna regret this, Jenise. You are going to be so sorry that you threatened me," he said coldly as he backed out of the room.

"The only thing I'm sorry about is that I didn't threaten your trifling butt sooner," she answered. "Now get out!"

Reggie did as he was told and ran out of the apartment.

Jenise dropped the knife and rushed over to Aaliyah. A large bruise was beginning to form on her tiny face. Jenise picked up the phone and dialed nine-one-one. When the paramedics and police arrived, she told them everything, no longer feeling the need or desire to lie to protect Reggie.

The next morning while Jenise was at work and Aaliyah was at school, Reggie returned to the apartment with his younger brother, supposedly to pick up his things. After they'd packed all of his clothing Reggie went into the kitchen and noticed the knife that Jenise had threatened him with the evening before. In a fit of rage, he took the knife and stabbed holes in the couch, the mattresses in the bedroom, and anything that he could find that it would penetrate. Then he and his brother proceeded to trash the apartment. In the kitchen, they took flour from the cabinets, ketchup and mustard from the refrigerator, and floured and painted all of the furniture with it. They dumped all of the food out of the cabinets and the refrigerator onto the floor. Then one by one, they smashed all of the dishes. They took all of Jenise's clothes as well as Aaliyah's clothes from their closets and dressers and piled them in the bathtub. Then they ran the tub full of water and covered everything in bleach. They kicked holes in the walls and smashed up the furniture, leaving it splintered in little pieces.

The first thing Jenise wanted to do when she came home and saw the state her apartment was in was to break down and cry, but she didn't. She called her parents and asked if she and Aaliyah could stay with them until she was able to find another place. Her father was so elated to know that she was finally separating from Reggie that he immediately came over with his pickup truck so that they could move anything that was salvageable. Jenise reported the vandalism to her landlord, and then they left.

One of the first things her mother told her when she arrived at their home was that she needed to get counseling. It wasn't easy walking away from a marriage, and Jenise had been through a lot. It didn't take much convincing before Jenise agreed to attend the meeting.

Jenise inhaled. Then she exhaled. Lastly, she pushed open the door and walked into the room. Although the meeting hall was located in the basement of her church, Jenise was surprised when she walked in to see that some of the women were from her own congregation. For some unknown reason, she had assumed that the ministry was set up for and attended by other women within the community. She'd never imagined that so many women in her own church were currently or had been the victims of domestic violence.

"Hello, Jenise."

She turned in the direction that the voice came from and was surprised to see her former third-grade Sunday School teacher Mrs. Grayson smiling at her. Mrs. Grayson was a wiry old lady with silver hair and cocoa skin who'd known their family since Jenise and Ellen were small children.

"Hi," Jenise answered nervously.

"Your first time here is always the hardest. Don't be afraid, and don't feel as if you have to talk. There are people here to listen if you want to share, but you don't have to do anything you are not comfortable with." She smiled reassuringly and led Jenise over to an area with chairs.

Jenise quietly took her seat and looked around the room at all of the women. Many were members of her church, and others were complete strangers. She immediately felt a twinge of apprehension at sharing her business with so many people. For a brief moment, she considered leaving. Then she remembered the heartbreaking sound of her child screaming when Reggie hit her and her bottom suddenly felt glued to the chair. She wasn't sure how it would help, but she knew that she had to stay.

The leader of the group was a black woman in her midforties named Claire. Jenise was immediately impressed by her demeanor, style, and obvious class. Her natural hair was cut in a short, curly afro with brown highlights. She was dressed casually in designer jeans and a nice blouse. Claire stood up and introduced herself, then welcomed everyone to the meeting. The very first thing she did after that was give the ground rules to put everyone at ease.

"This is a safe place, and above all else, we exercise discretion. Some of the ladies here are in hiding. Others have not found the strength to move out, and they go home to their abusers on a daily basis. For that reason, we have some basic rules that are designed to protect all of us. First of all, if you speak with your family, friends, babysitter, or whomever you talk to about where you will be on Tuesday evenings, you need to tell them you are attending a women's Bible Study group. That is a truthful statement as everything we do will be based on biblical principles and taken from our Bibles."

Claire told them in the past, word had gotten back to the husband of one of the attendees that his wife was attending domestic violence classes and he retaliated by assaulting her. There was a separate class held at the church for couples; however, that particular group was only for those couples who'd reached a point in their marriages that they wanted to work on their domestic violence issues together. According to Claire, unfortunately, the women in their group had not gotten that far yet. Therefore, their primary responsibility was to assist and protect each other. She went on to say that names were not mandatory but welcomed if you wanted to share. The most important ground rule was that everyone attending the meeting must agree to the utmost level of confidentiality. Nothing that was said or done during their sessions was to ever leave the room.

"If you are in hiding, or you feel that you are being stalked, or if your life is in danger, then please let the members of this class know. We encourage you to share a photograph of your husband with the group, so that if he is seen on the premises, we can make you aware and alert the authorities if necessary. Statics tell us that a woman and her children are often in much more danger from their abuser after they leave their home."

Jenise suddenly felt grateful that she was not in such a predicament. After his assault on their apartment, she had not seen or heard from Reggie and felt confident that she would not.

Next, Claire rattled off some startling statistics regarding domestic violence. "Every nine seconds in the United States a woman is assaulted or beaten. Around the world, at least one in every three women has been beaten, coerced into sex, or otherwise abused during her lifetime. Most often, the abuser is a member of her own family. Domestic violence is the leading cause of injury to women—more than car accidents, muggings, and rapes combined. Studies suggest that up to ten million children witness some form of domestic violence annually," Claire said.

Hearing that statistic made Jenise think of Aaliyah again. She made a mental note to ask if there was any type of counseling she could get for her daughter.

Claire continued. "Nearly one in five teenage girls who have been in a relationship have stated a boyfriend threatened violence or self-harm if presented with a breakup. Every day in the United States, more than three women are murdered by their husbands or boyfriends. Ninety-two percent of women surveyed listed reducing domestic violence and sexual assault as their top concern. Domestic violence victims lose nearly eight million days of paid work per year in the United States alone, which is the equivalent of thirty-two thousand full-time jobs. Based on reports from ten countries, between 55 and 95 percent of women who had been physically abused by their partners had never contacted nongovernmental organizations, shelters, or the police for help. The costs of intimate partner violence in the United States alone exceed five point eight billion dollars. Four point one billion are for direct medical and health care services, while productivity losses account for nearly one point eight billion. Men who as children witnessed their parents' domestic violence are two times more likely to abuse their own wives than sons of nonviolent parents."

Jenise was startled by the numbers. She'd had no idea how prevalent domestic violence was, or how costly.

As if sensing everyone's reaction, Claire spoke again to reassure them. "I know these numbers can be a bit frightening and overwhelming, but they are necessary. Most victims of domestic violence believe that they are alone in their pain and that no one could ever understand how they feel. The statistics prove that simply is not true. Everyone here has been abused by a loved one. You are not alone, and we do understand."

During the next phase of the meeting, Claire allowed the women there the opportunity to share their stories. Jenise shrunk down in her chair, praying that she would not have to speak. When Mrs. Grayson stood up to speak, her ears perked up. It was difficult for her to believe that the kindly old baldheaded gentleman she saw in service every Sunday was an abuser, and she was anxious to hear their story. Her suspicions were quickly proven wrong. Mrs. Grayson explained that she'd been abused when she was in her early twenties by her high school sweetheart. The two of them married after she became pregnant when she was only nineteen years old. Jenise could not believe how closely Mrs. Grayson's story resembled her own. Mrs. Grayson went on to say that she had two children with her first husband before she grew weary of the abuse and left him. After they were divorced, she married her current husband that Jenise knew at church.

She wasn't sure if it was proper protocol or not, but Jenise raised her hand to ask a question of Mrs. Grayson. "I left my husband and moved in with my parents," she said. "But I have to admit that I still love him, and I don't believe God condones divorce. Isn't there any other way?"

"Of course there is, sweetie," Mrs. Grayson answered. "What we do here is try to help you learn to deal with the pain you've experience with prayer and scriptures. As

Claire mentioned, we also have a couple's class for those who can get their husband to attend. We are not here to talk you into divorcing your husband. It's our sincere prayer that every marriage can be saved."

"While we are not promoting divorce, we also feel it's very important that each and every one of you realize that God does not condone domestic violence. Many women stay in abusive marriages because they believe that God wants them to. That is simply not true," Claire said. "The scripture tells us in 1 Peter 3:7, 'In the same way, you husbands must give honor to your wives. Treat your wife with understanding as you live together. She may be weaker than you are, but she is your equal partner in God's gift of new life. Treat her as you should so your prayers will not be hindered.'"

Instinctively Jenise had known that God did not approve of Reggie constantly punching, hitting, and slapping her, but she felt grateful to have actual scripture references to support that belief.

Another young woman who Jenise guessed was about her age raised her hand to speak. She also guessed that the woman weighed around 250 pounds. She told the group her name was Harmony; then she told her story.

"My husband and I were married for ten years, and we had three children. We had a beautiful four-bedroom home, a nice car, and an abundance of material things. Most people thought we were living the American dream, but I lived in an abusive relationship for most of that time. Don't get me wrong, it wasn't all bad. We had some good and even some great times. Often we could go months without an incident, but I still spent most days feeling afraid and apprehensive.

"After the first few times I learned the signs when it was coming. I could tell by the sound of his voice or the way he looked at me that an attack was about to happen.

"One time he punched my coworker right in the face because she gave me rides to work when he wouldn't. He told her if she ever came near me again, he'd kill us both. She had him arrested, but by dinnertime he was back home blaming me for it and knocking me around the kitchen.

"I grew up in a Christian home and believed that God could solve any problem, so the family joined a church together. We attended regularly, and he even became an usher. I foolishly believed that would be the end of our issues, but it wasn't. He'd get angry at me for putting too much money in the collection plate or coming home late from choir rehearsal. Once he even accused me of making eyes at the pastor during his sermon. I've taken many beatings as a result of trying to be involved with my church family.

"Finally, I moved into a shelter, and I filed a restraining order against him. The next thing I knew, I became an instant outcast among my church members. No one could believe that as big as I am any man could hit me and get away with it. My pastor called me and told me that I needed to get into joint counseling with my husband and learn how to forgive him. He told me that men have lots of pressures and that as the nurturer, it was my responsibility to ease those pressures and fix things. He told me that God wanted me to go home, so I did, and I became a victim all over again. During our ten-year marriage, I have had my nose broken twice, two ribs broken, and several lacerations over and around my eyes. I've suffered through busted lips, numerous dislodged teeth, and a dislocated shoulder.

I've also suffered broken bones that included my arm, my wrist, and my leg."

Harmony stopped talking and touched her bright red hair. Jenise thought the color was brash and looked unnatural.

"Some of you may notice that I'm wearing a wig," Harmony continued. "It's not a fashion statement. He set my hair on fire, and it never grew back completely. I still have several bald patches.

"For a long time I felt that there was nothing that I could do and that one day I was going to die at the hands of my husband. Then I found this group of women who welcomed me, cried with me, prayed for me, offered me solace, and have supported me without blaming me. I thank God for this group and for all of you ladies."

By the time Harmony was done speaking, Jenise had tears falling down her face. Quietly she bowed her head and prayed. "Thank you, God. Thank you for bringing me here."

At the end of the meeting, Claire gave them a list of books and other resources they could pick up for more information. She also gave out a list of Web sites and local agencies the women could visit. She told them that she hoped to see everyone again next week, but realistically she knew that some would not return for one reason or another. If that happened, she wanted to be sure that they knew where to find help when they needed it. When the meeting concluded, they all joined hands and prayed together for each other's safety, and then they were free to go.

As she drove down the street to her parents' home, Jenise was shocked to see two police cars parked in front of their house. Frightened, she jumped out of her car and rushed up to the front door. A police officer blocked her entrance.

"You can't go in there, Miss," the policewoman said.

"I live here. This is my parents' home. What's going on?" she asked.

Looking inside she noticed her mother and father sitting on the couch with two police officers questioning them. Her mother was staring sadly at the floor, and Jenise could tell that she was crying. Then she suddenly looked over and noticed Jenise standing in the doorway.

"That's my daughter. Please let her in," Deloris instructed.

Jenise rushed over to them. As soon as she did, she noticed a large bruise on the side of her father's jaw.

"Oh my God, Daddy, what happened to your face?" she asked.

"He got into a fight with Reggie," Deloris answered for him. "He came here demanding to see you, and when your father refused to let him in, they ended up in a fight."

Jenise's entire body suddenly filled with dread. "Aaliyah? Where's Aaliyah?" she asked.

Deloris slowly shook her head and tried unsuccessfully to wipe the tears from her face with a handkerchief. "He overpowered us both, and he took her. Reggie's taken Aaliyah."

The police officers tried to reassure Jenise that a Levi's Call Amber Alert had been issued, and that they were confident that Aaliyah would be found soon, but it did no good. All anyone could hear at that moment was the sound of Jenise screaming and wailing.

Chapter Fourteen

"What are you doing with my phone?" Semaj asked.

He'd just walked over to Gwen in the green room of the studio where Kandyss Kline's talk show was taped. Gwen was among the family members scheduled to speak on the show they were taping regarding Wayne's disappearance.

"This isn't your phone, it's mine," she replied.

"Are you sure? I could have sworn I left mine lying on this table."

Gwen looked at the screen and noticed that something was indeed different about her iPhone. She'd taken a photo of herself posing in front of a fountain in the park wearing her favorite pair of tight jeans with a red tank top. She'd set the photo as the screen saver for her phone, and it was no longer there. Confused, she looked across to the other side of the room and saw her mother chatting away on an iPhone. Suddenly she remembered giving her mother her phone to call their family to make sure they knew to watch them on TV. Guiltily she handed the phone to Semaj.

"I'm sorry. It looks just like mine," she said.

"No worries. It's an honest mistake," he said.

Semaj took the phone and walked out of the green room before Gwen could tell him about the phone call he'd just missed. He went down the hallway to the area where his private dressing room was located.

Rip was lounging on the couch waiting for him and eating fruit. "Did you find your phone?" he asked.

"Yeah, I'd left it in the green room," he answered.

Rip bit into a strawberry and swallowed the sweet fruit. "See, that's exactly what I mean about you not being cut out for this. When I was in the business, I never carried a cell phone. All I ever used were pay phones and pagers. They are a lot harder to trace."

"I have to have my cell phone for my work. I get tips from people via text message, e-mail, Facebook, and Twitter." Although they were alone in the room Semaj looked around before continuing. "Besides, there is nothing in my phone that could connect me to the disappearance of Wayne James."

Rip grabbed another strawberry and put it in his mouth. "That's not the point. The point is that we cannot afford to make any mistakes. Not knowing where your phone is at all times is a mistake. Mark my words."

"Yeah, well, there are not going to be any mistakes. I've got what I needed, and now it's just a matter of putting everything altogether."

Earlier that morning, Semaj opened his door to a FedEx delivery that contained the DNA results he'd ordered. After taking the package from the driver, he paced back and forth in his apartment feeling almost afraid to open it. For as long as he could remember he'd wondered who his father was, and now an envelope was in his possession that would answer that question once and for all, and he couldn't bring himself to open it up.

Semaj sat down on the sofa and held the envelope in his hand once more. As he did he thought back over his life and all of the times he'd regretted not having a father in his life. Pop Al was a great man, and a wonderful grandfather, but for Semaj, his presence in his life just wasn't enough.

When he was ten years old, his church youth group held a father-and-son camping trip. All of the boys were encouraged to bring their dads along with them. Neither Semaj nor Rip had a father to bring, so they asked Pop Al if he'd come along with them. Nothing in this world could make him disappoint his grandson, so he happily agreed. He closed the barbershop up early that Friday night and helped the boys pack up their gear and sleeping bags. They all kissed Semaj's grandma Nettie good-bye and told her they'd see her the next afternoon.

They met in the church parking lot, then drove out into the woods where they parked the vans and loaded their gear on their backs to walk the rest of the way. The half-mile hike to the campsite was extremely difficult for Pop Al. He was sixty-one years old, overweight, and a heavy smoker. Semaj cringed with embarrassment as he wheezed, huffed, and puffed his way along the trail.

Finally they arrived at the campsite, and Pop Al helped them unpack their gear and set up their tent. Afterward, the boys went down to the creek and fished for their dinner. Semaj was beginning to have a great time. Since Pop Al was one of the best fishermen in the county all of the boys and their dads came to him for help with everything from what type of bait to use to how to reel in their fish. With Pop Al's help, Semaj managed to reel in the biggest catch of the evening.

As they returned to the campsite, Semaj noticed that Pop Al was lagging even farther back than he had earlier. He and Rip stopped to wait for him to catch up.

"Are you all right, Grandpa?" Semaj asked.

"I'm fine. This cold air is just messing with my arthritis," he answered. He bent down and rubbed his aching knee. "I'll be all right," he said.

By the time they got back to the campsite, Pop Al was limping and barely able to move about. The youth leaders huddled all around looking at him with concern.

After watching him for several moments, Mr. Austin, the group leader, spoke up. "I'm sorry to have to do this, Mr. Matthews, but I think you need to cut this trip short and go on home. I'll have my assistant walk you back to the van and drive you back into town," he said.

Pop Al protested. "No, I don't want to disappoint the boys. I'll be fine. There's no need for anyone to make a fuss over me. Does anyone have any aspirin I can take? That will ease the pain."

"No, we didn't bring anything like that. Besides, I think you leaving would be best for everyone."

Although he didn't say it, Mr. Austin was seriously concerned with having such an old man along with them. The last thing he wanted to do was be responsible for his health further declining due to exposure to the weather and any other hazards they might encounter in the woods.

As he and Rip sat in the back of the van with Pop Al in the front and the assistant leader driving them back home, Semaj was livid.

"I can't believe he did this to me," he whined.

"He didn't do anything to you, Semaj. At least he came with us, and we got to have a little fun," Rip replied.

Semaj sighed. "He tried, I suppose, but if I had my own dad, this never would have happened. You just don't understand how I feel."

"Of course I understand. My dad wasn't there either. I had to borrow your grandfather because I had no one else to ask."

Glancing up in the front of the van Semaj made sure that his grandfather could not hear him. "He's good people, but he's still not my real dad. At least you know where your dad is, and you can even go to the jail and visit him if you wanted to. I don't even know my dad's name."

Rip didn't respond, so Semaj spent the rest of the ride home staring out the window and sulking.

As he grew up, he longed for a father-and-son relationship. When he'd finally found Wayne he thought his search was over. The irony did not escape Semaj that the one man he'd always felt was the perfect dad was the TV character Henry Forrester, played by Wayne James. Every Monday night, Semaj felt as if he'd practically crawled inside the television in order to spend time with his pretend dad.

He loved watching the episode when Henry's son Dwayne needed help with his science project, and the two of them built a working volcano with colored baking soda and vinegar. Since it was a comedy, of course, they ended up having it explode all over the kitchen walls. Semaj laughed and thought of how much fun it would be to mess up the kitchen ceiling with his own dad.

Another of his favorite episodes was when Henry and all three of the boys went on a ski trip in the Poconos. While sitting in the lodge sipping cocoa, they had heart-warming talks about how much they truly meant to each other. But the best one of all of the episodes that Semaj had seen was the one when the eldest of Henry's sons graduated from high school on the show. Wayne's character was sent out of town on business at the last minute and throughout the episode tensions mounted over whether he'd arrive at the auditorium in time for the commencement exercises. Semaj wanted to stand up in the living room and cheer when, just in the nick of time, as his TV son Rollo was stepping up to the podium to give the commencement address, he showed up and stood in the back listening and beaming with pride.

At his high school graduation, Semaj was also chosen as valedictorian, and he was assigned to give the commencement address. He'd buried his grandparents only two months prior so he knew that neither of them would physically be there. As he stepped up to the podium, wearing his royal blue cap and gown and carrying his speech in his hand, he looked out over the crowd. He realized it was unlikely and by some measures impossible, but he couldn't help but wish that at the last minute, and just in the nick of time, his father would show up and stand in the back row beaming with pride. Of course it did not happen, and Semaj went home alone that night and cried himself to sleep.

Daydreaming about having a father wasn't the only way the lack of a dad had affected him. After he moved to Atlanta and began to attend college, Semaj met and briefly dated a woman named Penny. She was his first real girlfriend, first serious relationship, and first sexual encounter. At the end of the semester, he and Penny broke up and she dropped out of school for over a year. When she returned, to everyone's surprise, she had a young son that she'd named Trevor.

Penny was a private and quiet girl and gossip soon began to circulate around the campus that Semaj was the father of her baby. Feeling confused, betrayed, and most of all, duped, Semaj stormed over to her apartment one afternoon and banged on the door.

"What are you doing here?" she asked when she opened it.

"I came to see my son," he said flatly.

Penny stared at him in disbelief. "What makes you think that you have a son living here?"

"Do the math, Penny. We broke up, you dropped out of school, and now you have an eight-month-old son. I didn't grow up with my father, and there's no way I'm going to allow my son to feel the same level of abandonment that I felt. Now let me see him."

Penny sighed loudly. She backed up slowly and allowed Semaj to enter. Once inside, he noticed a tall, dark skinned man sitting on the sofa, holding the baby in his lap.

"Who's this?" Semaj demanded to know.

The man stood up and handed the baby over to Penny. He extended his hand. "I'm Trevor. I'm Penny's boyfriend and the father of her son."

Semaj stared at him but did not take his hand. "You're his father?" he asked.

"Yes, I am. I overheard you at the door, and I'm not sure why you seem convinced otherwise, but I can assure you that Junior is mine."

Penny tried to explain that she'd met Trevor shortly after leaving school, and Junior had been conceived that summer. Her pregnancy was the reason she didn't return to school, but she assured Semaj that she wasn't carrying his child when she left. She also told him that Trevor Jr. was only five months old, not eight as everyone had assumed. Feeling ashamed and stupid, Semaj turned around and left.

If he really tried, Semaj could think of hundreds of similar incidents where the lack of growing up with his father had made him feel equally as ashamed and stupid. He reasoned that it wasn't fair. He was a good person with a kind heart who lived a moral life. He just couldn't understand why God has chosen to leave him without a father in his life.

That afternoon, unable to take the suspense or turmoil any longer, Semaj finally ripped open the envelope containing the DNA report and read the results. On the paternity results paper there were a lot of numbers and other items that he did not quite understand, but there was no mistaking one line. "Therefore, probability of paternity is 99.942 percent." Semaj didn't know whether to laugh or cry.

The fruit basket in the dressing room was almost empty as Rip continued to eat. "So you have your results, and now you are about to go out there and be interviewed by Kandyss Kline about the things you do in order to find a missing person. Do you mind if I ask what you plan to say?"

Semaj sat down in a nearby chair and pondered. "Well, I'll tell her that my first step is always to speak with the family and try to find out who saw the person last. That's where I find the most clues. Then I'll let them know that I go into the community and I start asking questions of the average person. Often these folks don't want to call in or be identified, but if approached correctly they will talk."

Rip nodded his head. "So how many days are you going to run around talking to folks while you pretend to look for him?"

"I haven't gotten that far yet, but it won't be too long. Just keep our guest comfortable until I get to him." Semaj stood up and began pacing again, anxious for his time to appear on camera.

Rip decided to change the subject. "Have you talked to Ellen?"

"Nope," he answered.

"You mean to tell me you still haven't called her after all this time?"

Semaj stopped pacing long enough to stare at Rip. "No, I haven't called her. What am I going to call her for?"

"Um, let's see, you can start by apologizing for acting like a jerk these past few weeks. Then you can tell her that you love her, and you can't wait to marry her. Then if that doesn't work, you can beg for her forgiveness."

Semaj continued pacing. "Do we have to go over this again? You are Ellen's biggest cheerleader lately. What's up with that?"

Rip watched him go back and forth before answering. "I'm worried about you, man," he said finally. "You've never appreciated the things that you have. Even when we were kids you thought your life was so bad. Yet, when compared to me and a lot of other kids, you had it great. Now you've found the kind of woman most men will only dream of and instead of doing everything you can to hold on to her, you're neglecting your relationship."

"Having my father in my life is very important to me. I may be a grown man, but I still need to have him acknowledge me. My life just won't be complete without it."

"That's exactly what I mean. You spend so much time focusing on the things that you think you don't have that you completely forget about all the things that you do."

A stagehand knocking at the door interrupted their conversation. He poked his head into the room. "Mr. Matthews, you're on next. I need you to follow me so that we can put your mike on."

Obediently, Semaj stopped pacing and followed him out of the room and down the hallway to the studio where the show was being taped before a live audience. The stagehand put the mike on Semaj and told him where to stand and wait to be introduced.

As he stood in the wings waiting, he heard Kandyss speaking. "Last year, the city of Atlanta was heartbroken as we learned that four-year-old Pierré Estefan Jenkins was missing from his mother's backyard. Three days later, he was found and returned to his mother's grateful arms by my next guest. He's the anchor for the seven o'clock news, but that's not his calling. Semaj Matthews has a God-given gift. Single-handedly, he's reunited dozens of families with their loves ones. I've invited him on the show tonight to give us his thoughts and insights on how to find our beloved Wayne James. Ladies and gentlemen, Semaj Matthews."

As he stepped onto the stage, Kandyss offered Semaj a seat directly beside Wayne's sons. Right next to him was Wayne's oldest son Stacy. The other four boys were seated next to Stacy in order of age. Jaden, Kelsey, Trenton, and the baby boy, Leo, were all there.

Semaj noticed that they all looked upset, sad, and lost. Trying to ignore their obvious pain, Semaj sat down and turned to focus on Kandyss.

After they exchanged polite pleasantries Kandyss began to ask questions. "So, Semaj, you've seen the police reports. Do you have any thoughts on this case so far?"

"Um, not really, Kandyss. From what I've read, the police do not have many clues so it's definitely going to be an uphill battle."

Kandyss nodded. "You're the best at what you do. I'm sure it will be easy for you."

"The police told us that if a person isn't found in the first twenty-four hours, the chances of finding them alive drops drastically. Is that true?" Stacy asked.

His question startled Semaj. He thought that he wanted to speak with Wayne's family, but now that he was there, it terrified him. Rather than look him in the eye, Semaj addressed the answer to Kandyss.

"In many cases that is the truth. However, I try not to be deterred by statistics. A few years ago, I found a woman who'd been missing for over ten years. She'd been taken as a small child and didn't realize the people who'd abducted her were not her parents," Semaj answered.

As the interview continued, Semaj loosened his necktie and tried his best to remain calm. At the insistence of Kandyss, each of Wayne's sons shared their favorite memory of time spent with their father. Semaj knew that she was trying to gain sympathy which could translate into high ratings for the show, but it was tearing him apart inside. He started to sweat under the hot lights, and all he could think of was getting as far away from the stage as possible. His head was swimming, and he felt that he might faint at any moment. He stared at the floor wishing it would open and suddenly suck him right in.

Kandyss turned to Wayne's oldest son Stacy to ask how he felt about his dad and what his most memorable moment was.

"Well, it's really not a memory at all as I was too young to actually remember it, but the best thing about him is that he took me and my brothers into his home and gave us a father. I ended up in the foster care system when I was six months old because both of my biological parents were arrested for running a meth lab out of our apartment. Wayne took me in as his foster son, and then my biological parents relinquished their parental rights and I became his forever. I can't remember it, but that was the best day of my life."

Unlike his brothers, Stacy knew who his biological parents were and had contact with them. They knew he'd been adopted, and both were still spending their time in and out of jail for various crimes.

"Have you been in contact with your biological parents during this ordeal?" Kandyss asked.

"No, I don't see a reason to. Yes, they gave me life, but Wayne James is my father. It takes a lot more than biologically creating a child in order to earn that title."

His words permeated Semaj's heart and were swirling around deep inside his soul. He looked into the young boy's eyes realizing he had tons of wisdom packed into his seventeen-year-old body.

Kandyss scooted closer to the edge of her chair and poked her microphone into Stacy's face. "Tell us, Stacy," she said. "This audience and my viewing audience at home are anxious to hear what you feel makes a man a father."

"That's simple," he said matter-of-factly. "The only way to be a true father is to imitate our original Father, God. In the Holy Bible, we find that there are almost forty verses in the scripture about God's heart for the fatherless. He protects them, He provides for them, and He defends them. We are called to be imitators of Him. That's not what my biological parents have done, but it's what Wayne James has done for me and my brothers. It's what I will do for my own sons."

The audience began to applaud wildly, and Kandyss waited for the fervor to die down before she spoke again.

"So, I take it that you plan to have lots of children of your own someday with your wife," she asked.

"That would be ideal for me, but if I don't have biological sons, then I know that I can still be a father. Dad has taken us throughout the community and taught us about mentoring other young men. I have a twelve-year-old mentee whom I currently consider to be my son. Most people don't realize this, Kandyss, but being a father isn't biological; it's spiritual. Wayne James was spiritually appointed by God to be our father."

The roar of applause from the audience filled the entire studio. Semaj felt like a fool. He was ashamed of his actions, and he felt deeply humbled. Feeling unworthy to look Stacy in his face, Semaj went back to staring at the floor.

"Mr. Matthews, can you please help us find our daddy? We just want him to come home again."

Suddenly looking up, Semaj realized that the question had been asked by Trenton, Wayne's nine-year-old son.

Unable to control himself Semaj burst into tears. "I promise. I promise I won't sleep until your daddy is home." He ran from the stage and snatched off his microphone. Still crying, he rushed into the dressing room and collapsed onto the couch beside Rip. "What have we done, man? Those kids are missing their father just like I did when I was their ages, but the difference is I caused their pain. I caused all of their pain."

Rip shook his head. He'd believed from the very beginning that Semaj was too soft and would eventually crack under the pressure. It was typical behavior. Semaj never hurt another person in his life, and no matter how he felt about Wayne James, he didn't want to hurt him or his children either. He knew this day was coming. He'd seen the signs a mile away. Sitting beside his cousin as he cried his eyes out, he couldn't help but be thankful that the Semaj he knew seemed to finally be on his way back.

Chapter Fifteen

After his meltdown at the television studio Semaj went home that night intent on putting the pieces of his broken life back together. He could not believe how obsessed he'd allowed himself to become regarding having a father in his life, when the thing he'd been searching for was right there all along.

The morning following the show, he called Ellen. He knew that he had to apologize and fix their relationship. She didn't answer the phone, so he left a detailed message.

"Honey, it's me, Semaj. First, let me just say that I am sorry. I have been acting like an idiot for weeks. I've been mean to you, and you didn't deserve it. Please, please, forgive me. You are the best thing in my life, and you make me a better man. I'm on my way to Andrus for the day, but I'll be back later tonight. Please call me as soon as you get this message. I love you."

He hung up the phone and called Rip.

"Hey, man, how soon can we put an end to this ridiculousness?" he asked.

Rip sat down on his sofa and cradled the phone on his left shoulder. "You've got to give yourself at least forty-eight hours. If you rush in and supposedly find him today, it will look suspicious. I mean, especially after the way you broke down on television last night."

Semaj smiled. "That wasn't a breakdown, brother. It was a breakthrough. Finally, I am seeing everything clearly."

"I'm glad to have the cousin I know and love back. Are you going to talk to Ellen today?"

"I wanted to, and I called her, but she didn't answer. So I'm going to Andrus. I need to visit Pop Al's grave."

Leaning back on the sofa, Rip's ears perked up. "What's that all about? I mean, didn't you stop by the cemetery when we were there a few weeks ago?"

"Yeah, but this is different. I need to," Semaj paused. "I need to apologize to him."

"Apologize? What do you need to apologize for?"

Searching inside of himself, Semaj tried to find the words to explain to Rip how he was feeling about his late grandfather. As he was growing up, he had a great relationship with his grandmother Nettie. She was in many ways his best friend, his confidante, and for all intents and purposes, his mother. Because he'd always known that Allison was dead, he didn't long for her, and therefore, he was easily able to accept the maternal love of Grandma Nettie. His grandfather was a different story. He loved him, he respected him, he confided in him, but he never ever accepted him as his father. He was Grandpa, Pop Pop, Poppa, and Pop Al, but Semaj never allowed him to be his father. The fact that Pop Al did everything a father would do had been completely lost on him until he sat onstage listening to words of wisdom from the seventeen-year-old son of the man he'd kidnapped. He tried his best to articulate those feelings to Rip.

"So that's why I want to go to the cemetery and let him know that I was wrong. It's just like you said years ago. I had the best dad in the world, and I didn't even realize it. Not only that, he knew that one day he'd be gone and I'd still need a father, so he gave me the gift of the Heavenly Father. He taught me to know and believe in God, the Father to the fatherless."

Rip waited to respond as he realized that Semaj was crying on the other end of the line. Silently he allowed him to release his emotions.

"Trust me, Semaj. You don't need to apologize. I mean, if you feel it's something that you need to do for yourself, I fully support you. But I gotta tell ya, I don't think it's necessary. He was not only a good man, but he was very insightful. He understood."

Wiping his tears on the back on his hand, Semaj nodded. "You're probably right, man. Hold on a sec, I got a call coming in on the other line." Semaj quickly clicked over. "Hello?"

"Semaj, it's Ellen."

His feelings of joy that she'd called him back quickly dissipated after he noticed the panic and fear in her voice. Sobbing between words she told him that Reggie had taken Aaliyah from their parents' home the night before.

"Calm down, baby, you're going to start hyperventilating. Take a deep breath and just slow down."

Ellen inhaled and exhaled rapidly. "I know things have not been right with us, but we need you. You are the best at finding missing persons. Please, Semaj, will you help us?" she pleaded.

Her words let him know that she had not listened to his apology message, but Semaj didn't care. He decided that he would explain everything in person.

"I'll be right there," he said.

He arrived at Ellen's parents' house a short time later after instructing Rip to go to the warehouse and check on their "guest." He climbed the porch steps two at a time and rang the front doorbell.

Jenise rushed to the door and let him in. "Semaj, I'm so glad that you are here. I've never been as worried in my life as I am right now."

Semaj greeted Ellen's parents first, then walked over to give Ellen a hug and kiss. He was taken aback by her cool attitude toward him. Then he remembered that he had not yet apologized to her face to face. As much as he wanted to, he realized that the time was not right. Jenise commanded his complete attention. She stuck a photograph in his face.

"This is the most recent picture of Aaliyah that I have," she said.

Tentatively, he took the picture from her. "I don't think I really need a picture. I know my soon-to-be niece when I see her." He glanced over at Ellen, who was sitting on the sofa by her parents, to check her reaction to his statement.

"That's right. I'm sorry. I'm just a bundle of nerves right now. I guess I wasn't thinking," Jenise answered. She took the picture back. "Just tell me what you need from me."

He put his arm around her shoulder and slowly led her over to a chair to sit down. Then he sat down next to her, took out a pad and pencil to begin taking notes, and started to speak. Suddenly, he stopped and turned to look at everyone.

"Mr. and Mrs. Winston, Ellen, Jenise," he said, "I know that one of the main reasons that you called me was because I'm considered the authority in Atlanta on finding missing persons. I assure you that I'm going to do everything in my power to find Aaliyah, but if you'll just bear with me a moment, there's something I have to say before we get down to business."

They all looked at him expectantly waiting for him to speak. The words came out quickly as Semaj bared his soul. He began by explaining to them all how he'd always felt inadequate for not having a father growing up. Next, he explained that a few weeks prior he'd found out the identity of his biological father with the help of Gwen. He apologized to Ellen and assured her that there was nothing going on between them. He admitted that he'd been acting like a different person and not focusing on his work or the things that were most important in his life.

Malcolm spoke up and asked him if he would tell them who his father was. Without hesitation he told them that it was Wayne James. He suddenly stopped explaining when he realized that he would implicate his cousin Rip if he also told them that they were responsible for Wayne's disappearance. He reasoned that his involvement was a secret he'd have to hold on to for just a little while longer.

"Regardless of all that, I want everyone here to know that my focus right now is on finding Aaliyah and bringing her safely home." He turned to look at Ellen. "We are getting married in a few months, and there's no way we can do that without our flower girl, right, honey?" Nervously he waited for Ellen to respond.

Without giving him an answer, Ellen ran over and jumped into his arms covering him with kisses.

"I'll take that as a yes," Semaj smiled.

Ellen returned to her seat, and Semaj turned to Jenise to get down to the business he knew best.

"Jenise, I need to get as much information from you as possible about Reggie. I need a list of his friends, his family, the places he likes to hang out. Anything that you can tell me will help in getting Aaliyah back quickly."

"Reggie is secretive. I don't know the names of any of his friends. His mother lives near Dunwoody. That's where he works on his music. He has a studio in her basement. The police have already been there, and his brother said that they haven't seen him for several days."

Semaj scribbled notes onto his paper. "Give me the address. His family might not be telling the truth."

"They are lying through their capped teeth," Malcolm said. "He was driving his brother Jermaine's car when he left here with Aaliyah."

"What kind of car is it?" Semaj asked.

"It's a 2004 Toyota Camry," Jenise answered.

Semaj wrote down the make and model of the car. "Does it have any distinguishing marks or dents on it?"

Jenise thought for a few seconds. "The last time I saw it there was a dent on the back bumper. I doubt that Jermaine ever got it fixed because he already spent the money he got from the insurance company."

"We've given all of this information to the police, and they still have not found her," Deloris said suddenly. "I know you are good at what you do, Semaj, but this whole situation is tearing me apart. She could be screaming for help right now," she cried.

"Reggie's a wife-beating jerk, but he's still Aaliyah's father. I don't think he'd hurt her," Semaj told her.

Ellen looked over at Jenise, and she nodded her head giving her permission to tell Semaj everything. "The night that Jenise moved out, Reggie came home in a rage. He hit Jenise, and when Aaliyah tried to call for help, he attacked her too."

That piece of information shocked Semaj. Ellen had confided in him early in their relationship about how abusive Reggie had been to her sister. The entire family had tried to convince her to leave, but she would never listen. However, the one bright spot that any of them saw in her marriage was her daughter Aaliyah. As far as any of them knew, Reggie was a good father, and his little girl adored him. He could not imagine what type of fear and rage had filled him to make him strike her. More than ever, the situation took on an overwhelming urgency for him.

"Don't worry. We are going to find Aaliyah and get her back home. I promise."

Semaj was doing his best to reassure them, but he feared that his words were falling on deaf ears. They knew how dangerous Reggie could be, and they all were worried sick.

When he was done collecting information, Ellen walked him to the front door. He leaned down and kissed her on the lips.

"Is there anything that we can do to help?" she asked.

"Pray," Semaj said before turning to walk away.

During the next couple of days he used all of his resources to search for Reggie and Aaliyah. He went to pay a visit to Reggie's mother, but she was not at home. Instead, his brother answered the door. The same as he'd lied to the police when they visited earlier that week he lied to Semaj. He assured him that neither his brother nor his niece was there.

"Eyewitnesses say that he was seen driving your car on the night he abducted Aaliyah. What do you know about that?"

Jermaine thought quickly and came up with a lie. "I told you I haven't seen him in over a week. The last time I saw him, I let him take the car. He hasn't been back here since."

He felt confident in his lie because he'd parked the car out of sight.

Semaj fired off several more questions at Jermaine. When he left he was convinced that he was lying, but there was little that he could do about it. Although the Atlanta police had issued the Amber Alert, Semaj knew from experience that they were not making finding Aaliyah a priority. Parental abductions amounted to a large number of missing children, and unfortunately, they received less attention.

On a hunch, Semaj decided to knock on the door of the home next door and ask questions. The woman at the house didn't have much information to give him, but Semaj gave her his business card and asked her to give him a call if she came up with anything.

That hunch was beginning to pay off two days later when Semaj received a phone call from the neighbor, Shelly.

"Hey, Mr. Matthews, I have some information that might help you find that little girl you're looking for."

Semaj was at his computer going through the comments section on one of Reggie's online videos looking for clues as to where he might have gone.

"I'm glad you called," he said. "What can you tell me?"

"Well, I didn't see the little girl, myself, but my daughter did. When I got home from work today, she told me that she saw Aaliyah playing in the backyard this afternoon. She said that she walked over there and asked if they could play together, and then Aaliyah's dad came out and got her and took her back inside."

Filled with excitement Semaj could hardly contain himself. "Are you sure it was Aaliyah?" he asked.

"Yep, my daughter is sure. They played together almost every day last summer."

Semaj thanked Shelly, then hung up the phone.

Chapter Sixteen

Reggie parked his brother's car in front of one of the buildings in Sand Poole Manor and hopped out. "Aaliyah's asleep. Just keep an eye on her until I get back," he instructed his baby brother.

"Hurry up, man. We need to get out of Atlanta," Jermaine answered. "Why don't we just go back to the house?"

"We can't go back to the house. You know Momma started tripping after she found out about that Amber Alert Jenise had put out. That's crazy. How can you kidnap your own child? Then Momma started talking about turning me in. I can't believe she threatened to call the police on her own flesh and blood. There's no way I would ever go back there after how she treated me. So just chill until I get back."

Reggie trotted through the parking lot into the breezeway, and then knocked on the apartment door of the first apartment on the left.

"Wassup, Reggie?" his friend DeAngelo asked.

"Hey, man, I need your help. I'm looking for a place to lie low for a while."

DeAngelo stuck his head out the door and looked first to his left, then his right, and back to his left again. When he was positive that no one else was around, he invited Reggie into his apartment and closed the door.

"What's going on with you? The word on the street is that you beat up Jenise and trashed your apartment. That doesn't sound like you at all."

Reggie was grateful that his reputation in the neighborhood was still intact. "Of course it doesn't. I mean, we had a little fight, but Jenise has blown this mess way out of proportion. She's staying over in Buckhead with her parents."

DeAngelo reached for his remote control and pressed the button to pause the basketball game he'd been watching on television. "So if she went home, then why don't you do the same?" he asked.

"That heffa has called the cops, and there's a warrant out for my arrest. I went over to her parents' house to talk to her about it and get her to drop the charges and things got out of hand. My mom is seriously tripping, and I just need a place to crash for a few days." Reggie paused. "To be honest, I need a place where the cops won't find me."

DeAngelo shook his head. "That's gonna be hard to find around here. Ever since Rip went legit, the city's been on a quest to clean up this whole project. You know the cops drive through Sand Poole Manor every half hour. You can't hide out here."

Reggie looked around and rubbed his hands trying to think. He'd come to DeAngelo because prior to Rip's sudden departure from the drug game, DeAngelo had been Rip's right-hand man. After Rip testified, the DEA did a clean sweep of the projects, and everyone involved in his business dealings went to jail. Most of them were only given a few years jail time, but for a brief time, there was not one drug dealer left on the street. That is, except for DeAngelo. No one really knew why, but Rip had shown him complete loyalty, and his name was not brought up. He'd never been arrested or even questioned. He still lived in the same luxury apartment that he'd lived in while working for Rip. Reggie had never asked him how he made his money, but he was pretty sure he knew the answer.

"Look, man, I know you can help me. It doesn't have to be here at Sand Poole, but you've got to have somewhere that you can let me hide out. I'm begging."

DeAngelo picked up his remote again to restart the basketball game. "Why should I, Reggie? I mean, you are my boy and everything, but I just don't like the sound of this whole situation."

"What if I pay you? I don't have any money on me right now, but as soon as all of this is over, I'm going to be signing a record deal. That's why I can't go to jail right now. My career is finally about to take off."

DeAngelo was anxious to get back to his basketball game, and he was tired of dealing with Reggie. He didn't believe his career was going anywhere, but if it did, he figured he could cash in on the investment.

"Fine, I don't have an apartment, I do have a place where you can hide, but it's pretty basic. There's no running water or electricity. It's just an old abandoned warehouse located way out in Alpharetta."

"I'll take it," Reggie replied eagerly.

DeAngelo walked into his bedroom to retrieve the keys to the back door. He returned and gave them to Reggie. Then he sat down on his sofa and picked up a pen and piece of paper.

"Let me write down the address for you. It's way off the beaten path," he explained. "Do you know your way around that area?"

"My brother's car has GPS. I'm sure we can find it."

DeAngelo stopped writing and looked up at him. "Your brother is with you? I thought you were alone."

"Um, no, I don't have my own car so I borrowed his." Reggie stopped talking and DeAngelo noticed that he looked guilty.

"Is that all?" he asked. "I feel like you aren't telling me everything."

"I'm telling you everything there is to know. I just need a place to hide for myself. He's going back home after he drops me off," he lied.

DeAngelo finished writing the address down on a piece of paper. He handed it along with the keys to Reggie, who read over the address, then turned to DeAngelo. "Are you sure this place is safe?" Reggie asked.

"I'm positive. Back in the day, Rip and I used this warehouse for storage. After, well, you know, everything went down, we were able to get our stash out, and the police never knew about it. To be honest, nobody knows about it but me and Rip. So when you finally leave, bring me back the keys. Then you need to forget that you were ever there. Do you understand that?" DeAngelo looked him straight in the eye.

"Yeah, man, I hear you."

By the time Reggie got back to the car Aaliyah was awake and crying.

"It's about time you got back," Jermaine said. "This brat will not shut up. I know she's your kid, but you should've left her where she was."

"Shut up!" Reggie said. He climbed into the driver's seat, then turned around to look at his daughter. "Aaliyah, baby, what's the matter?" he asked.

"I want my mommy," she whimpered.

"Sweetheart, I told you that Mommy is sick right now and she can't take care of you. You're gonna be staying with me for a while."

Aaliyah wiped her tears on the sleeve of her T-shirt. "Then I wanna go back to Granny Murphy's house."

"We're going back there in just a little bit. First, we are gonna go to McDonald's and get some chicken nuggets. Won't that be fun?" he lied.

Starting to perk up, Aaliyah nodded her head.

"You got money for McDonald's?" Jermaine eyed him suspiciously.

Reggie ignored him and started the engine to the car. "Don't worry about that. I got us a place to stay tonight. It's a warehouse way out in Alpharetta. After we get settled you can go out and get us some food."

"I thought you said this guy could find us a decent place to stay. A warehouse is not decent." Jermaine smacked himself on the forehead. "This is ridiculous. I don't even know why I agreed to come with you."

Listening to him whine, Reggie began to wonder as well. If it wasn't for the fact that he desperately needed his car, and Jermaine was reluctant to let him leave with it alone, Reggie probably would not have bothered to bring him.

As he drove he tried to make sense of the nightmare that his life had become in just a few short days.

When his mother asked him, he had told her the truth. Yes, he'd hit Jenise. She got on his nerves sometimes, and he hit her. It wasn't like his dad had not knocked his mother around on a regular basis. Sure, he was a minister, but he also was the sole authority in his house and anytime his mother dared step out of line, he quickly put her in check. He also admitted to her that he'd trashed the apartment in anger. Jenise had no right to pull a knife on him, he reasoned.

After that incident at the apartment, Reggie went home to his mother and while working in his studio he decided that he was glad to be rid of Jenise. It wasn't that he didn't love her. He honestly did. It just appeared to Reggie that since she'd gotten pregnant and he'd been forced to marry her, his life had gone steadily downhill.

He was excited about his impending contract with Curtis Jansen. Reggie knew that he was a talented singer and songwriter. Whenever he sang at churches around the Atlanta area he was able to make old ladies in big hats fall out in the Spirit. His songs had a classic R&B feel to them that also made young people jump to their feet clapping and lifting their hands in praise. Reggie loved the feeling it gave him to know that his audience was enjoying the music that he made. He reveled in the glow of applause.

Although he got paid a generous salary, Reggie had hated the years he spent as musical director at his father's church. It wasn't easy teaching words and parts to what he considered to be a group of untalented misfits. With hard work and a lot of yelling, he was actually able to make them sound good, but it was a hollow victory. The last place Reggie wanted to be was behind a piano or even standing in front of the choir with his back to the audience. Reggie believed that he deserved to stand alone on the stage. He didn't believe that he was just any old ordinary singer. In his mind, Reggie was a superstar. That belief was the primary reason he'd stopped singing duets with Jenise. Her voice was too strong and passionate, and often, she stole the show. After they performed, it made his blood boil if she received more compliments than he did. He'd told her that he felt that she should concentrate on raising Aaliyah instead of having a music career with him. Jenise was a doting mother so she agreed without much protest. The truth was he really didn't care what type of mother she was. He simply did not want to share the spotlight with anyone, especially his wife.

While driving he thought back to the day earlier that week when he had been in his studio in his mother's basement putting the finishing touches on his latest track and Jermaine knocked on the door interrupting him. Feeling annoyed that he had been bothered, he opened the door anyway.

"I'm busy, Jermaine. Make it quick," he snapped.

"The cops just left here. They were looking for you."

Reggie quickly pulled his brother into the sound-proof studio. "Why are the cops looking for me?" he asked after they'd both sat down.

"Jenise said that you beat her up and smacked Aaliyah. They also said you vandalized your apartment. They had three warrants with your name on them."

In all their years of marriage, Jenise had never reported the abuse to law enforcement. Reggie was shocked and livid.

"What did you tell them?" he demanded.

"I didn't tell them anything. I said that you didn't live here and I had not seen you in a few days. They gave me a card and told me to call if I heard from you."

Reggie breathed a sigh of relief. "That's good." He patted his brother on the back. "You are very smart, little brother. That will give me some time."

"Time to do what?" Jermaine asked.

"I need to borrow your car. I'm going to go over to her parents' house and talk to Jenise. I'm sure if I apologize and sweet-talk her, I can get her to recant her story."

Jermaine shook his head. "Nope, I need my car for work. Anyway, can't the police prosecute you for domestic violence even if Jenise doesn't cooperate?"

"They can try, but without her testimony, their case won't stand a chance. I won't be gone long. I'll be back before you have to leave for work."

Jermaine stood up to leave. "Jenise's parents don't like you very much. Just call her on the phone."

"I can't call her. She cut off my cell phone. If I use your phone or the house phone she might tell the police where I am. Listen, I know my wife. Face to face, there is no way she'll say no to me."

Jermaine was still reluctant to turn over his car keys. He really didn't have to go to work that evening. He just really believed that what Reggie was planning was a very bad idea. It wasn't until his brother reminded him that he had helped him trash the apartment and could also be charged that he finally relented.

When he arrived, taking Aaliyah was the furthest thing from Reggie's mind. That is, until he ran up against a brick wall named Malcolm Winston. As soon as he saw Reggie through the screen door standing on his front porch he became infuriated.

"Get out of here, you trifling no-good bum," he yelled.

Reggie held up his hands in front of himself. "I don't want any trouble. I just want to see my wife."

"She's not here. Even if she was, I still wouldn't let you see her. Your days of tyranny ruling over my child have ended. Now get your worthless, cowardly behind off of my porch before I throw you off."

Being insulted enraged Reggie. He snatched open the screen door, breaking the latch. Then he stormed into the house. "Where's my wife?" he bellowed.

"I told you she's not here."

Malcolm grabbed him, and the two men tussled with each other. Their wrestling match became rougher, and both men ended up on the floor. Malcolm was winning and had almost gotten Reggie to an angle where he felt he'd be able to push him back out onto the porch. Then Reggie swung his fist, hitting Malcolm squarely in his jaw and knocking him unconscious on the floor. Reggie stepped over him and began going through the house screaming, "Jenise! Jenise!"

He walked from room to room becoming more agitated with each step because he could not find Jenise. He finally stormed into the kitchen and discovered Deloris and Aaliyah huddled in a corner trying to hide.

"Give me my kid!" he ordered.

When Deloris did not comply, he walked over to her, violently pushed her down onto the linoleum floor, and snatched Aaliyah out her arms.

At that point he had no idea what he planned to do with her as he was acting purely on rage-filled adrenaline. All he knew was that he wasn't allowing her to stay in a house where he'd felt disrespected.

Three days later, his mother threatened to turn him in to the police if he didn't return Aaliyah to her mother. So he'd blackmailed his brother into leaving with them.

"Stop daydreaming. You just missed your exit," Jermaine said.

Reggie looked up and realized his brother was right. In the distance he could see the golden arches, and he realized he had not eaten since earlier that morning.

"Let's go ahead and get something to eat, then we'll turn around."

Back at his apartment, DeAngelo was sitting on his couch cheering for the Boston Celtics to wipe the floor with the Atlanta Hawks. Since he wasn't a fan of the local team, he enjoyed watching the game alone in the privacy of his home. That way he didn't have to explain or argue about his preference.

A commercial came on, and he walked into the kitchen to get a snack. He took out the wheat bread, a pack of turkey, some sliced cheese, and mayo. He slowly made himself a sandwich, then grabbed a beer from the fridge. When he returned to the living room he noticed that the basketball game had been interrupted by a news bulletin.

"A Levi's Call, Amber Alert has been issued in the Atlanta area for a five-year-old African American girl. Aaliyah Breasia Murphy was taken by force three days ago
from her grandparents' home. Both of her grandparents were assaulted during the abduction. She was last
seen wearing blue jean shorts, a grey Minnie Mouse
T-shirt, and pink tennis shoes. Murphy was taken by
her father Reginald Tyrell Murphy. Due to a past his-
tory of violence as well as his assault on his daughter's
two elderly grandparents, Mr. Murphy is considered to
be extremely dangerous. He was seen leaving the area
driving a 2004 red Toyota Camry. If you see him or his
vehicle, you are asked to call the police immediately."

As the reporter read the story, DeAngelo saw a photograph of Aaliyah and Reggie on the screen. He dropped
his plate on the table.

"That jerk just lied to me," he said aloud.

He stared at the TV for a few moments trying to
decide what to do. When he'd agreed to help Reggie
he had no idea that he'd taken his daughter. Hitting
his wife was one thing. Taking a child was a horse of
a different color, and DeAngelo could not afford to be
involved in that. Besides that, he didn't feel an abandoned warehouse was a safe or sanitary place for a
small child to be staying. He picked up his cell phone
from the coffee table and dialed.

"Hey, man, I need your help," he said into the phone.

"What's up?"

DeAngelo hesitated before answering. "There's a
problem with the warehouse out in Alpharetta."

Rip listened intently as DeAngelo explained; then a
big grin spread across his face. "Hey, don't worry about
it. I'll handle it," he said, then hung up. He immediately
dialed Semaj's number. "Tonight's the night. I need
you to meet me at the warehouse."

Since his appearance on Kandyss's show, his entire focus had been to locate Aaliyah. Semaj had completely forgotten about Wayne James still being held at the warehouse. As much as he wanted to rescue Wayne and bring closure to his sons, he sincerely felt that finding Aaliyah took precedence.

"I can't tonight, man. I just got a lead on Aaliyah's whereabouts. I need to head to Reggie's mother's house. She was seen there earlier this afternoon."

"They are not there anymore," Rip answered.

Semaj was just leaving his apartment when he received the phone call. He opened his car door and got in. "Have you seen them? How do you know that they are not there?" he asked.

"There's no need to go after the prey. He's about to walk right into our trap and at the same time send Wayne home to his sons."

"Stop talking in riddles and explain, Rip."

While he sat in his car, Semaj listened to Rip explain their new plan.

"I just got off the phone with DeAngelo. Reggie had stopped by there earlier tonight. He is on the run with Aaliyah and his brother. DeAngelo sent him to hide out at the warehouse, and when he gets there he will definitely stumble onto Wayne James."

"Are you saying that we let him find Wayne and call the police, then we are free and clear?" Semaj asked.

"In a perfect world that might work, but you've forgotten two things. Reggie is running from the police, and he has Aaliyah with him. The last thing he's going to do is call the police."

Semaj leaned his head back on the headrest. "There's no way we can go back there to feed Wayne or let him go if Reggie's there too. This is not good news at all."

"Like I said before, you are not cut out for this kind of work. Let me explain it to you. We go out to the warehouse, we call the cops, and tell them Reggie's there. They show up to arrest him and coincidentally find Wayne James. Aaliyah goes back to Jenise where she belongs. Reggie goes to jail where he belongs. Wayne James is free to return home to his sons. Semaj Matthews continues to be Atlanta's hero."

Shaking his head Semaj argued. "Haven't we done enough already? Do we have to frame Reggie for kidnapping Wayne?"

"Who said anything about framing him?" Rip asked indignantly. "The police can draw whatever conclusions they want. We are not going to say he did anything."

"Okay, smart guy. How do we explain why you and I were at the warehouse to find Reggie there?" Semaj asked.

Rip pondered the question for just a few seconds before coming up with a brilliant plan. "You just told me you got a tip about her being at his mother's house. So we'll say that based on that tip, we decided to trail him, and he finally stopped at the warehouse."

Hesitation and dread settled in Semaj's spirit. He didn't know why, but he was sure that something was terribly wrong with their great plan.

"I don't know, man. Something about this just doesn't feel right."

"Then what do you propose that we do? Reggie is on his way to the warehouse right now, and at any moment he's going to discover Wayne. We can't stop that from happening. I'm proposing a way for you to keep promises that you've made to Jenise and to Wayne's family. Do you really want to gamble on Reggie doing the right thing?"

Semaj started the engine on his car. "I'm on my way." He hung up the phone and sped out of the parking lot.

Chapter Seventeen

Wayne sat listening to music in the warehouse. For reasons that he had not yet figured out and didn't totally understand, a couple of days after his abduction his captor had gone to immense pains to make his captivity more comfortable. The idea that you could be kidnapped and comfortable at the same time was an oxymoron, but Wayne realized that while he didn't know who'd grabbed him or why, it definitely wasn't a savage.

Instead of being tied to a hard wooden chair, the captor had provided him with a cot for sleeping. He'd untied the ropes on his hands and feet and instead, shackled his ankles to the cot with a long chain. The cot was subsequently chained to the wall preventing it from moving. It made Wayne feel as if he were a St. Bernard or Labrador in someone's backyard. There was only so far that he could go before the chain stopped him. Nevertheless, he was grateful to be able to stand, sit, and move around on his own volition whenever he wanted to.

In order to avoid boredom, the abductor also provided Wayne with a small battery-operated clock radio, while warning him that he should turn it on sparingly because once the batteries were dead, he would not replace them. The red digital numbers on the clock were all of the light that Wayne had seen since he was abducted, yet he reveled in it like sunshine. In order to preserve his batteries he only turned the radio on once per day for a few moments in the evenings in order to listen to the news and a little bit of music.

Wayne was also dumbfounded by the fact that each afternoon his captor brought him food. Due to the circumstances he expected to be thrown scraps or barely edible rations. Instead, his meals were nutritious and surprisingly delicious. It pained him to admit that it was some of the best meals he'd ever eaten in his life. He'd assumed that in order to protect his identity his captor would not buy food from a restaurant. Yet it boggled his mind that the same person who'd gagged and dragged him from his condo was apparently standing in front of a stove on a daily basis to cook for him.

The entire situation was both frightening and intriguing. At times he felt like Paul Sheldon from the Steven King novel *Misery*. It was obvious that his captor wanted to treat him with care, and at times, he wondered if he'd been taken by an overzealous female fan. The few times that his captor spoke he knew that the individual was using a voice distorter, and that could be utilized by anyone. Running different situations through his mind and playing out different scenarios as the reason for his capture helped Wayne to pass the time.

He put his hands behind his head and lay back on the cot as he continued listening to the news. Most nights his abduction was mentioned and it made him feel hopeful to know that he had not been forgotten and people were looking for him.

Lying there quietly he unexpectedly thought he heard his son Stacy's voice. He sat up quickly and looked around at the darkness. His heart was racing as it had been weeks since he'd seen his children, and he missed them tremendously. Suddenly he realized that the voice was coming from the radio. He slid closer to it, and listened intently to the sound bite from his son's appearance on Kandyss Kline's talk show several days prior. He beamed with pride at how his son had handled himself under the pressure.

The next voice he heard surprised Wayne. It was Semaj Matthews, who was also a guest on the show. Wayne realized they'd called the best reporter in Atlanta to help look for him, and he felt grateful. As he listened he heard Semaj make a promise to his sons to bring their father home. His words humbled Wayne and made him ashamed.

He's looking for me, and I treated him like crap, he thought. *I don't deserve a son like him. I never did.*

Wayne closed his eyes and went back over thirty years to the night he met the beautiful, vivacious, and captivating Allison Matthews.

Wayne stood onstage staring out into the audience as they jumped to their feet and cheered. The star of the play, Kip Saunders took his third bow and basked in the glory.

"What a ham," Wayne whispered to the girl standing next to him on stage. "I bet he smells like bacon."

The two of them giggled under their breath until the curtain finally closed and they were free to walk off the stage.

"We're going to Pizza Hut, are you coming?" Kip yelled to Wayne as he walked offstage.

"No, thanks, I have to get home," he responded.

"Suit yourself," Kip replied. He put his arm around two of his beautiful costars and sauntered out of the backstage area.

Wayne looked at him with disgust. It wasn't that he didn't like Kip; he just didn't like the circumstances that they always seemed to end up in. Wayne knew he was a better actor, but because he was black and Kip was white, their drama teacher always gave him the lead role in every play their high school presented. Wayne, on the other hand, ended up with a small part playing a neighbor, a waiter, or other insignificant character that barely had three lines. It was a tired and well-worn story in his hometown of Lawrenceville, North Carolina. The only black students who got any respect at his high school were the athletes. Wayne didn't run, jump, or tackle anyone, and he didn't plan to. Yet, he knew he was a talented actor, and he was intent on proving it to the world.

"All of this is going to change as soon as I get to Chicago," he said loudly to himself as he was walking through the parking lot to his car.

"What's gonna be so different up there?" a sexy female voice drawled.

Wayne turned around and looked into the most beautiful face he'd ever seen in his life. She was leaning against a dark blue Mustang with one hip poked out in his direction. Her dark brown eyes sparkled in the moonlight. Wayne could not help noticing that she had a round face with the kind of cheeks that made him want to reach out and pinch them. As he watched her, she pulled a rubber band out of her pocket and pulled her long hair back into a ponytail.

"Um . . . Everything's different up north," he answered. As much as he tried he could not take his eyes off of her.

"You sound like a runaway slave." She laughed heartily at him, and in spite of himself, Wayne laughed also. He extended his hand to the enticing stranger.

"I'm Wayne James," he said. "I've never seen you around here before."

She popped loudly on a piece of gum. "That's 'cuz I don't live around here. I'm visiting my cousin for the weekend. I'm Allison." Lightly she shook his hand.

"Where are you visiting from, Allison?" he asked.

"Andrus, South Carolina."

Wayne smiled at her. He couldn't help enjoying the way her lips moved when she chewed and popped her bubble gum. She blew a big bubble, then sucked the air back into her mouth causing it to deflate. With just a few words he'd become mesmerized by the way she spoke with a sexy Southern twang.

As they stood in the school parking lot and talked for the next hour Wayne learned that Allison was an only child, she loved reading mysteries, and she was a cheerleader at her high school but only during football season because basketball was boring in her opinion. He also learned that her favorite food was hot dogs with chili. Her favorite TV show was Sanford & Son, and even though she hated it with a passion, she'd been playing the piano since she was eight years old. She also told him that she was in town spending the weekend with her cousins who were Wayne's classmates.

He told her that he was the youngest of four. His mother had two boys and two girls, and they all graduated from college and were successful educators. His brother was a high school math teacher. His older sister taught third grade, and his younger sister earned a degree in early childhood education and operated a day care center. Wayne let her know that he had no intention of ever teaching school. Instead, he dreamed of being a famous actor like Richard Pryor or Sidney Poitier. After his high school graduation, which was coming up in few weeks, he planned to move to Chicago to pursue his acting career. When Allison asked *why not New York City or California he didn't really have an answer. He stated it was just the largest city he'd ever been to and it seemed like a good place to start. He knew it didn't make a lot of sense, but he was determined to give it a try.*

They went out on their first date the next night, and by the time she left on Sunday afternoon to return to Andrus, Wayne knew that he was head over heels in love. They wrote each other daily, and she returned for frequent visits.

Two weeks after his high school graduation, Wayne was due to board a bus headed to Chicago and his acting future. He couldn't bear to go without Allison.

"Marry me and come to Chicago," he begged.

Allison happily agreed. Her parents had other ideas. They told Wayne that they were both too young to be so seriously involved and that there was no way that they would give their permission for her to get married. Also, because of their disapproval of the relationship, they forbade Allison to return to North Carolina for visits with her cousins.

None of that mattered, and a week later Allison and Wayne eloped, and Wayne took a job working in a local tire plant. Their plan was for them to save enough money for both of them to move to Chicago together. Allison was deeply in love, and she fully supported every aspect of Wayne's career.

A little over a year later Semaj was born. They christened him Wayne James, Jr., and the three of them settled into life in Lawrenceville.

Then one night Wayne came home from his job at the tire plant furious. Although he'd worked there for over a year, the company had hired someone else to come in and be his supervisor.

"It's not fair," he told Allison. "I work my tail off, and nobody appreciates it."

"Forget them, Wayne. You know what? Forget that job too. You were not born to be a supervisor in a tire plant. You have a God-given talent for acting, and you are wasting your talent while working at that plant. It's not your calling."

Wayne lay his head on her shoulder as they sat on the used couch they'd purchased at a thrift store. "I know, but what choice do we have? We have a son to feed. I can't just quit."

"We have savings. Let's just take the plunge and go to Chicago. If we sit around here waiting one day you'll wake up and our son will be twenty years old and you'll still be dreaming about having a career. Worst of all, you'll blame me for taking your dreams away."

Wayne didn't believe that he would ever blame his beloved Allison, but he agreed that he didn't want to look back over his life and have regrets. The next day, he put in his two-week notice and quit his job.

Their savings were not enough to pay for the bus tickets and rent an apartment, so Allison went to social service to apply for assistance for her and her infant son. When they asked about her husband, she lied and told them he'd left her. With the government's help, they were able to rent a tiny one-bedroom shack in a horrible neighborhood. It wasn't much, but it was theirs. No matter what, they believed they could survive anything as long as they were together. Wayne worked a bunch of part-time jobs while he searched for acting gigs.

Living in North Carolina the two of them had experienced what they believed to be winter, but neither of them was prepared for the down-to-the-bone chill *that whipped through them by the Chicago winds known as the Hawk. Late one evening they sat shivering on the living-room sofa. The radiator was on, but their raggedy house was not well insulated and there were cracks in the windows. Allison had Semaj wrapped tightly in blankets huddled up against her.*

"I'm freezing," she said with her teeth chattering.

"I'm going to walk down to the store and get some duct tape. If I put it on those windows that will help us stay warm," Wayne answered.

"We'll go with you," Allison said.

Wayne shook his head. "No, honey, it's too cold for you guys to be outside tonight. Just bundle up on the sofa, and I'll be back soon."

He'd never found out how the fire started that killed his wife. As he came walking up the street, all he saw was the crowd of people gathered in front of his house as smoke billowed up into the sky and flames shot out through the windows. He heard the scream of fire truck engines in the distance coming closer. He dropped his bag and broke out into a sprint for his home.

Rushing into his living room, he found his son lying on the living-room sofa still wrapped tightly in his blanket. He picked him up, rushed outside, and put him in the arms of the first person he saw standing on the street. He ran back inside to look for Allison. He screamed her name, but there was no answer. Coughing and wheezing, he headed toward their bedroom. He saw her lying facedown in front of the doorway. He ran toward her but instead of moving forward, he felt himself being pulled back.

"It's too late," a voice said. Wayne felt hands around his waist as a firefighter tried to pull him out of the burning structure.

Wayne tried to move forward again, and then screamed as the bedroom door frame collapsed from the fire and fell on top of her body.

Three days later, Wayne woke up in a hospital where he'd been taken for treatment of severe smoke inhalation. Confused, he looked around the hospital room trying to remember what had happened and how he'd gotten there.

"What happened to me?" he immediately asked his nurse when she walked into the room.

"You were injured in a fire, but you're gonna be okay," she answered. "There's a story about you on the news. Would you like to watch it?" she asked.

Still feeling confused, he turned toward the television set. A heavyset black woman was on the screen speaking to the reporter.

"This stranger came running past me, and he went in the house. He came back out carrying the baby, and he put him in my arms. Then he ran back in. When the firemen pulled him out again, he was unconscious. I guess he tried to save that poor girl, but it was too late. I was still standing here when they brought her out in a body bag."

Wayne burst into tears as the memories came back to him and he remembered that Allison had died in the fire. After several moments he wiped his tears and turned to the nurse. "Where's my son?"

The nurse looked at him strangely. "What son?"

"The baby that was taken out of the house fire, where is he?"

She shrugged her shoulders and left the room.

When he was released from the hospital Wayne realized he had no home to go to. He didn't know where his son was, and his wife was dead. Despondent, he called his mother. Thankful to hear from him she filled him in on the information she'd gotten from Allison's cousins. She told him that after the fire, the authorities had contacted Allison's landlord. She'd told them that Allison was a single mother with no family in Chicago whose husband had left her alone with the baby. They contacted her parents in Andrus, and they flew to Chicago to claim her body and take the baby home with them.

"It's time for you to come home, son," she said.

After hanging up the phone she sent him a one-way bus ticket back to Lawrenceville.

Wayne returned down South determined to get his son back, but Semaj's grandparents were not willing to give him up.

"You married her, got her pregnant, then you walked out on her," Alvin screamed at Wayne as he stood at his front door begging to see his son. "There is no way you are taking our grandson too. You are a worthless piece of crap, and we don't ever want to see your face around here again. If it wasn't for you, Allison would be alive today."

Wayne tried to explain that she'd only pretended to be separated in order to get assistance, but that only angered him more.

"I can't believe you are standing here saying that our daughter lied because you weren't man enough to support her. Is that supposed to make me feel better?" he bellowed."If you were half a man, you'd have gotten a good job and supported my daughter and our grandson, but you didn't. Instead, you were running after some pipe dream of being an actor. Get away from my house. You disgust me!" Alvin said before slamming the door in his face.

Walking away feeling as worthless as his father-in-law accused him of being, Wayne began to believe that he was right. If he hadn't complained about his job at the tire factory Allison never would have insisted they move to Chicago, and she'd still be alive today. His mother told him to fight. As her husband, he was Allison's next of kin and legal guardian of his son. But Wayne didn't have any more fight left in him. His marriage license and Semaj's birth certificate had gone up in smoke. No matter what anyone said, Wayne blamed himself for Allison's death. He wasn't worthy of her loyalty and love, and he certainly wasn't worthy of raising his son.

As he lay on his cot consumed with the memories of his past, Wayne suddenly heard a noise and voices. He reached over and turned his radio off, and then he sat quietly listening. His abductor had already brought his daily meal, and Wayne wondered why he would return. He heard the sound of a door opening and unfamiliar voices.

"Help me! Help me, please!" he screamed.

Chapter Eighteen

Earlier that evening, Wayne and Rip had pulled into the empty warehouse parking lot. "Turn your lights off," Rip told Semaj. "It looks like we got here before Reggie, and I don't want him to notice us when he pulls in."

Semaj noticed a secluded spot near a tree. He pulled over to it and parked the car as far out of sight as he could.

"This should be good. His lights won't point in this direction when he pulls in," he said as he turned off the engine.

Semaj didn't know why, but he was shaking like a leaf blowing on a tree.

"Calm down, you're making me nervous," Rip said.

"Shhh, I see lights in the distance," Semaj answered.

Rip laughed loudly. "We're inside a car over a hundred yards away. They can't hear us talking. But, you're right. That's the red Toyota. Call the police."

Nervously, Semaj dialed 911. He told the operator who he was and advised that he'd located Reggie.

"Is the little girl with him," the operator asked.

Semaj looked in the direction of Reggie's car as he slowly parked. He waited for them all to get out. "Yes, I see her and another man."

"Don't approach them, Mr. Matthews. An officer is on the way," the operator instructed him.

After he hung up, Semaj felt as if everything was happening in fast-forward motion. Although he was standing right there, the entire incident felt as if he was having a weird out-of-body experience. Instead of being involved in the action, he felt as if he were standing outside of himself and watching a movie.

Before he knew it, the police had pulled up and surrounded the warehouse. With lights and sirens blaring they were able to get Reggie and his brother to surrender quickly. The two of them were handcuffed and placed in the backseats of waiting cruisers while Aaliyah was placed in Semaj's waiting arms.

The police opened the bay door in the front of the warehouse and just as quickly they found Wayne James shackled to the cot. After using bolt cutters to free him, they brought him out.

Holding a shivering Aaliyah in his arms, Semaj tried his best to keep his distance from Wayne as he was led to a waiting police car. His attempt at being inconspicuous failed, and Wayne spotted him.

"Mr. Matthews!" he yelled.

Reluctantly Semaj turned in his direction. Wayne motioned for the policeman that was escorting him to follow him to where Semaj stood.

"I'm sorry to bother you, but this officer told me that you are responsible for finding me and this young lady," Wayne said.

"Yeah, I guess I am," Semaj answered with no emotion.

Wayne grabbed his hand and vigorously shook it. "I just wanted to say thank you. I am eternally grateful to you for what you've done."

The feeling of satisfaction Semaj had dreamed he'd have when he finally heard those words did not happen. He didn't feel elated. He didn't feel vindicated.

All that he felt deep down within was overwhelming shame.

"There's no need to thank me," he mumbled. Unable to look Wayne in the eye he pulled his hand back and stared awkwardly at the ground.

"I have to express my gratitude. I owe you my life," Wayne said.

Semaj looked up as he heard Ellen scream his name. She and Jenise had just arrived and were walking swiftly in his direction.

"No, you don't. You don't owe me anything," he told Wayne. He quickly walked away and rushed over to reunite Aaliyah with her mother.

As he drove Rip home that night Semaj felt conflicted and confused.

"What's wrong, cousin?" Rip asked.

"I don't know. I thought that I would feel better after this whole ordeal was over, but I don't. There's a gnawing knot in my stomach that won't go away."

"You don't have to worry about framing Reggie. I overheard the cops talking. They don't think Reggie kidnapped Wayne. They realize he's too big of a moron to pull off something like that. Can you believe he was asking them if he could collect the reward for finding him?"

Semaj laughed loudly. "No, you have got to be kidding. Does he realize he's going to jail for aggravated assault, vandalism, and kidnapping of his daughter?"

"This nimrod asked them if he could collect it and use it for bail."

The two of them howled with laughter. One of the things that Semaj loved most about his cousin Rip was that he could always find a way to cheer him up.

"I saw you talking to Wayne," Rip said after the laughter died down. "You looked pretty tense. What did he say to you?"

"He wanted to thank me for leading the police to him."

"A few days ago, that's exactly what you wanted. All you could talk about was making Wayne James owe you a debt of gratitude. How did it feel to finally get it?"

Semaj gave his cousin a look that he knew would explain exactly how he felt. Ever since they'd been kids they had a unique way of communicating with each other. They talked a lot, but often, no words were needed. They rode the rest of the way home in silence.

As soon as he was inside his apartment, Semaj picked up the phone and called Ellen. He'd just seen her when she and Jenise picked up Aaliyah from the warehouse, but he wanted to hear her voice again before he fell asleep.

"Hey, beautiful," he said.

"Hey, handsome," Ellen answered. "I can't tell you how proud I am to be your fiancée right now."

"Oh yeah? And why is that?" Semaj stretched out on the bed as he talked.

"You are amazing, Semaj. Not only did you find my niece and reunite her with our family, but you stumbled upon Wayne James too. You are all over the news, baby. I mean, it's not just Atlanta news either. You're on CNN," she gushed.

Wayne sat up on the bed. He no longer felt relaxed. "You know I don't like all the publicity. I just enjoy what I do."

"I know, baby, but you found a major celebrity that was missing. Whether or not you like it, this is a very big deal. By the way, did you get a chance to talk to Wayne James?" Ellen asked.

"Briefly, why do you ask?"

"Didn't you say that you found out he's your biological father? I guess I'm being silly. Of course, standing out there in the parking lot was not the place to discuss it."

"We discussed it before he went missing," Semaj said quietly. "He denied it completely, but I'm sure of it. I guess he doesn't want me in his life."

Ellen sighed. "Oh, sweetie, I'm so sorry. I guess that's why you've been acting so out of character lately."

"I suppose so, but I've accepted it. I mean, it would've been wonderful to have the great Wayne James as my dad, but it's not what he wants. I'm sure he's got his hands full already with five boys."

He stretched out on the bed again. As he lay there he explained to her how he'd had a breakthrough while taping *The Kandyss Kline Show*. Without revealing his part in Wayne's disappearance, he let Ellen know that he finally realized what being a father truly is, and that he'd had it all along.

"When you and I have kids, I promise you, Ellen, I'm going to be the best dad. I had a great role model in my Pop Al." Anxious to change the subject he continued, "First, we gotta jump that broom. Where are we with the wedding plans? I hope you didn't cancel everything all ready."

"No, I didn't cancel anything," Ellen assured him. "But we do need to choose our wedding menu with Cedric."

"I thought you took Jenise."

Explaining her personal meltdown, Ellen let him know that the menu was still on hold, but Cedric had agreed to set up another tasting as soon as they were ready. "If he can fit us in, do you think we can go next Thursday for lunch?"

"Sure, set it up, baby," Semaj said.

They spent a few more moments telling each other how happy they were that things were back on the right track, and they were eagerly looking forward to their big day. Then they finally hung up.

"We have got to stop meeting like this," Cedric's front-desk greeter joked when Ellen arrived at his catering service the following Thursday. "It's a pleasure to see you again, Miss Winston."

Ellen smiled broadly. "It's great to see you again too."

"Where's your busy fiancé today? I bet he's out finding more missing persons. Tell him I need him to find Elvis for me," he said obviously joking some more.

Laughing lightly, Ellen played along. "You know he can find anyone."

"When I saw on the news how he found your niece and Wayne James being held captive together in the same warehouse I was just in awe. He is simply remarkable."

"Thank you, so much." Ellen beamed with pride. "I just came from work so he'll be meeting me here soon."

Cedric came out into the waiting area to greet her. "Ellen, you're here," he happily exclaimed.

"Yes, I'm here again, Cedric." She hugged him warmly.

Cedric looked around. "Don't tell me that I'm still not going to get to meet your fiancé, the hero?" he asked.

"Oh, don't worry. Semaj will be here this time. We're excited about getting married and ready to grub on some good food."

Forty-five minutes later she was still sitting alone in the front lobby feeling like a complete fool. Several times she'd dialed Semaj's number, but he did not answer. Ellen was livid that once again he was missing appointments and not returning phone calls. After he explained to her about finding his father and how it was the reason for his erratic behavior she truly believed that they were well on their way to putting their relationship back on track again. Since that time, Semaj had seemed to her to be back to his old self. She kicked herself for actually feeling sorry for him when he'd told her that Wayne James cruelly rejected him. Apparently that was not the reason for his behavior since he was still missing appointments and ignoring her calls.

The clerk sadly looked at her with pity in his eyes. He didn't speak, but Ellen knew he thought she was as dumb as a box of rocks for continuing to put up with Semaj.

Finally feeling fed up, she stood up to leave just as her cell phone rang. She answered quickly, hoping it was Semaj.

"Hello," she said.

"Where are you?" Jenise asked frantically.

Ellen sighed. "I'm sitting at the caterer's waiting for Semaj, but I was just about to leave because it's obvious that he has stood me up once again. I am so sick of him acting like a crazy person. How many times is he going to say I'm sorry and expect me to just accept it? Even the Bible says that God doesn't forgive us unless we are truly repentant. Semaj obviously has not changed one bit so he can keep his sorry to himself."

Rattling on in anger Ellen did not notice that Jenise was not speaking. She had a lot of pent up anger inside, and she continued ranting and raving for several moments before she finally stopped.

"Jenise, are you still there?" she asked anxiously.

"I don't know how to tell you this, but Semaj is not coming. He can't come."

Suddenly Ellen noticed the urgency in her sister's voice. "Oh my God, what's going on? Is he okay?" she frantically asked.

"He's been arrested, Ellen. Semaj is in jail."

Chapter Nineteen

Wayne stood on the tarmac at the Atlanta airport anxiously waiting for the plane to touch down. He'd been in Atlanta for several weeks prior to his abduction, so it had been over a month since he had seen his five boys. Immediately following his release the week before he'd talked to each of them by phone, but they were in Los Angeles. Hearing each of their voices made him long to see them again. He'd been away from them for as long as he could stand and any moment they would be walking down the steps of the private jet he hired to fly them to town and walking into his arms.

Trenton was the first to step off the plane, and he bolted across the lot into Wayne's waiting arms. The other boys rushed out just as fast. When they all jumped on him they almost tumbled to the ground in a pile. Wayne sincerely wished he had more arms as he tried to hug them all at once.

"I have missed you guys so much," he said.

Squeezing tightly, he was filled with so much joy he didn't want to ever let them go. When they were finally able to bring themselves to break the six-way embrace, Wayne and his sons got into a waiting limousine and rode to the new house Wayne had rented in North Atlanta. His work required that he remain in the city for another three months, but he'd decided that he had spent too much time away from his sons and wanted them with him. He hired tutors for them so they could continue their education and rented a home large enough for them to come to the city and stay with him. It was a two-story home, with an open floor plan, four bedrooms, three bathrooms, two fireplaces, two balconies, underground parking for four cars, and expansive views of downtown and midtown Atlanta.

As he sat on the sofa later that evening, Wayne was elated to hear the sounds of family all around him. His boys were upstairs unpacking their suitcases and organizing their bedrooms. They were all very loud and boisterous, and the noise that they made was music to Wayne's ears.

"Hey, Dad," Jaden said.

Wayne turned around as his fifteen-year-old son came bounding down the stairs and walked into the living room.

"Trenton and Leo are arguing because they don't want to share a room," Jaden said. "Can we switch out? Let Trenton share with Kelsey and I'll move in with Leo."

Surprised, Wayne looked his son up and down trying to figure out what his motive could possibly be for volunteering to share his room with a four year old.

In their home in California, each of the boys had their own room. On such short notice Wayne wasn't able to find a six-bedroom home that he liked. Since there were only four bedrooms, he'd had to assign some of the boys to share. Of course, Wayne had his own room, and as the oldest, so did Stacy. In choosing the other roommates, Wayne thought it was best to group the boys by age. He assigned Jaden and Kelsey to share, and Trenton and Leo. Sitting quietly, Wayne pondered the idea for a moment of switching them around. Trenton and Leo were the two youngest boys, but Trenton and Kelsey were actually closer in age, with Kelsey being eleven and Trenton being nine. Pairing those two seemed as if it would work much better, and Wayne was about to agree. Then he remembered his original concerns.

"Okay, I understand that you don't want to share your room with your eleven-year-old brother, but why in the world would you want to live with a four year old?"

Jaden looked guilty but didn't say anything. He stared sheepishly at his feet.

"I'm waiting for an answer, young man," Wayne said.

Jaden walked over to the sofa and sat down by his dad. "The truth is, whenever you're home, Leo likes to climb in your bed at night. He rarely sleeps in his own room. During the day, he spends most of his time playing, and this house has a playroom. I just felt that sharing with him was the closest thing I'd get to have my own room here in Atlanta."

Wayne chuckled at his son's logic. "You are right about that. Sure, go ahead and switch. It's not a problem at all."

The next two boys to come rumbling loudly down the stairs were Kelsey and Trenton. They'd just been informed that they were now roommates, and they had lots of questions, like could they take the bunk beds apart and make them twin beds. Since Kelsey liked Batman and Trenton loved Spider-Man they also wanted to know if they could decorate their room with both. They also wanted to know if they could sleep on the floor in their sleeping bags that night because they planned to build a fort with two chairs and a blanket.

Laughing heartily and basking in the joy of having them around him again, Wayne agreed to everything they requested without putting up a fuss.

That night, Wayne walked from room to room to say good night. As always, he sat on the side of their individual beds, and he allowed each one to choose a Bible verse they'd like to read. When they were done, they prayed together, and he tucked them in. This was a ritual he'd begun with Stacy when he was only two years old, and he'd continued it as the boys grew older. He started in Leo and Jaden's room. Then he moved to Kelsey and Trenton, and finally Stacy. He tucked them all in, including Leo, who he encouraged to stay in his own bed for the night, although he suspected that he would not.

Returning to the living room, Wayne decided to watch the nightly news. The lead story shocked him as he sat staring in disbelief at the screen. He turned up the sound so that he could hear the reporter better.

"Atlanta's favorite son, Semaj Matthews, was arrested earlier this week and charged with kidnapping in the abduction case involving Wayne James," the reporter said. "As we first reported, Mr. Matthews led police to the abandoned warehouse stating that he'd located abducted four-year-old Aaliyah Breasia Murphy. When police arrived they also discovered Wayne James who was being held in the same warehouse. Sources within the police department who spoke on condition of anonymity have advised us that the discovery apparently was not a coincidence. Atlanta police believe that Mr. Matthews and his accomplist not only had prior knowledge that Mr. James was there, but that they are the ones who'd been holding him captive.

"Also charged in this case is Marion 'Rip' Sawyer. Mr. Sawyer made headlines a few years ago when his apartment in Sand Poole Manor projects was raided by DEA agents who suspected him of running a large drug ring. He was shot several times by the agents, but subsequently recovered from his injuries. Mr. Sawyer did not receive any jail time for that incident following his testimony. Stay tuned to this station for more information on this breaking news story."

Wayne was stunned. He could not believe what he'd just heard. After he was rescued he'd spent several hours at the police department answering questions. They told him that they did not believe the guy they'd arrested was the same person who had imprisoned him. Reggie Murphy was wanted on separate charges. He'd consequently been arrested and jailed.

Although he was anxious to see justice be served, Wayne was thankful to be free and didn't lose any sleep wondering who was responsible for his abduction. He'd given the police detailed information on his time as a captive, as much as he could remember. After they'd told him he was free to go he had not spoken with anyone at the department again.

Early the next morning, Wayne decided to go to the police department and get some answers. This whole situation had been confusing, and for the life of him, he couldn't fathom why the same man who'd saved him was now accused of committing the crime. He didn't know Semaj very well, but he believed that he was an honorable man. After all, Wayne reasoned, he had his blood running through his veins. He was his son. Brushing aside how badly he'd treated him, Wayne simply refused to believe that Semaj was guilty of anything beyond being the victim of extremely overzealous police officers with overactive imaginations.

He was escorted into a private meeting room as soon as he arrived. Quietly he sat waiting for a detective to speak to him. After about fifteen minutes, a short, stocky black man walked into the room and introduced himself.

"I'm Detective Sheffield. It's a pleasure to meet you, Mr. James. I'm the lead investigator handling your kidnapping case."

Wayne politely shook his hand. "Excuse me for just showing up like this, but I saw on the news that Semaj Matthews was arrested for my abduction. I don't mean to sound ungrateful, but how did you come to that conclusion?" Wayne asked.

"The perpetrator we arrested that evening gave us information that connected Marion Sawyer to the warehouse. I'm sure you are not aware of this, Mr. James, but Marion at one time was responsible for a large amount of drug traffic in and out of the city of Atlanta. After years of work, this department finally had enough evidence to arrest him, but the DEA took the case over. He gave up the names of his suppliers and a few other people, and the DEA allowed him to walk."

Detective Sheffield stopped talking and pulled out a pack of cigarettes. "Do you mind if I smoke?" he asked.

"Actually I do. Can you just finish answering my question?"

The detective put the cigarettes back in his pocket and continued talking. "I've been trying to get Sawyer off the street since that time. He claimed to have gone legit, but I knew it was just a matter of time before he'd slip up."

Wayne tried his best to ignore the smug smile that was plastered on the detective's face. "That still doesn't explain why Semaj Matthews was charged. What evidence do you have that connects him to the crime?"

"To be honest with you, we don't have a lot. The most compelling thing is that Sawyer is his cousin, and the two of them were together the night you were found. Matthews is the one who called the cops and led them to the warehouse. We are still working on the case, and we should have all the pieces of the puzzle together soon. There's nothing for you to worry about."

"I'm not worried," Wayne shook his head.

"That's good. While you are here, I need to go over something with you from your statement that wasn't clear." Detective Sheffield flipped pages in his folder. "It says here that one day your abductor stuck a stick down your throat. Do you know what kind of stick it was? Was he trying to make you gag?"

Wayne tried to remember that day the detective was speaking about. "It didn't go down my throat. If he'd had a flashlight I would have thought he was examining my mouth. He ran it along my teeth and over the inside of my cheek."

As he said those words, Wayne suddenly had a flashback of the incident. The flashback triggered another memory from several years prior.

Being a celebrity who adopted children from the foster care system Wayne felt that he experienced lots of joys and blessings. It also had a downside. It opened him up to scams and people looking to make a quick buck. His oldest son, Stacy, knew that his biological parents were in jail. Jaden's mother was in a mental health care facility, and his father did not want the responsibility of raising him, so he signed away his rights. Leo's mother was a prostitute that died shortly after his birth from infection. She'd delivered him while homeless and on the street without any medical care. Kelsey's parents were a different story. He'd been taken away from his mother after child protective services deemed their home unfit. It was infested with roaches and rats. Kelsey slept on a dirty mattress on the floor surround by human feces.

A year after his adoption was final, Wayne's lawyers received a phone call from a man claiming to be

Kelsey's biological father. In an extortion attempt, he demanded that Wayne pay him to go away. Wayne wanted him to go away, but he also wanted to make sure that he didn't bother them again. He didn't believe for one moment that the man was really Kelsey's biological father, so he requested a DNA test. After their nightly Bible study and prayer, Wayne had swabbed Kelsey's cheek. When he asked the extortionist to give his sample, he left town with no forwarding address.

All at once, Wayne came to the realization that his abductor had not tried to strangle him with a stick or examine his mouth. He'd swabbed his cheek for a DNA sample. He felt like rocks were rumbling around in his stomach as he realized that no one but Semaj would want to do that.

Detective Sheffield was asking Wayne another question, but he was not listening. He interrupted him mid-sentence.

"Are the culprits still in custody?" Wayne asked.

The detective shook his head. "A judge granted them both bail a few hours after their arrest. I don't think either of them is a flight risk, though. I've just got a few more things to clear up with you."

Wayne left the office abruptly without allowing him to finish. He began walking toward the front entrance, then suddenly noticed a swarm of reporters camped outside. Instead, he asked a police officer to lead him out the back way. When he finally arrived at his car, Wayne tried to leave but realized his hands were trembling and sweaty. He sat still for several moments trying to collect his thoughts.

Since he realized that a DNA test had been done, he was sure that Semaj now knew that his denial was a lie and that he was indeed his biological father. It astonished him that Semaj had gone to such drastic measures as kidnapping in order to obtain his proof. Yet, it also shed light as to the reason his abductor had not treated him cruelly. The only thing that Wayne did not understand was Semaj's actions when he was released. When he'd tried to thank him, he noticed that Semaj acted very distant toward him. At the time, he attributed it to their earlier meeting when he'd denied Semaj's paternity. Now he realized that Semaj knew that truth, but he had not confronted him or demanded he admit the truth. Instead, he'd allowed Wayne to walk away and kept the personal information totally to himself. After speaking with the detective, Wayne also realized that he had no idea of his connection to Semaj. Apparently he had not talked upon being arrested. Regardless of what he had done, Wayne could not help but continue to believe that his son was still an honorable man.

Wayne grabbed his phone and called Gwen.

"Hey, cousin, I need your help," he said cheerfully.

Gwen could not hide the surprise in her voice. It had been years since he called her personally. Usually, they communicated through his publicist or personal assistant. Immediately, her senses began to detect that he was about to feed her some bullcrap.

"Hey, Wayne, wassup?" she asked.

Hearing the apprehension in her voice, Wayne decided that it was time for him to come clean with her.

"You were right, Gwen. Semaj Matthews is my son. I'm sorry I lied to you. Can you please forgive me?"

His admission did not surprise Gwen one bit. His apology, however, did.

"You don't owe me an apology, Wayne. I'm not your son. It's Semaj that you need to apologize to."

"You're right. That's why I'm calling. I need your help in contacting him."

Sighing loudly, Gwen felt horrible being in the middle. "It's too late. Didn't you hear that he was arrested? His attorney is not going to let you say anything to him at all."

"I don't care about his attorney. My son is innocent, and I need to talk to him. There has to be a way for me to reach him. Give me his address. I'll just go see him."

Gwen was surprised once again by Wayne's sudden protection of Semaj. It didn't make sense to her at all. "You don't sound anything like the man Semaj and me were talking to at your hotel a few weeks ago. Why the sudden change of heart?"

"Let's just say I spent a lot of time alone thinking," Wayne said quietly.

It didn't seem possible, but Gwen was sure that she could feel his remorse emitting through the phone. "The truth is, Wayne, Semaj is no longer in Atlanta. Because of the publicity surrounding this whole thing he got special permission to leave town. I'm sorry. I don't know exactly where he went."

"Thanks, Gwen," Wayne said.

He hung up the phone and called his personal assistant, Leah.

"I'm going out of town for the day. Please take care of the boys for me. I should be back late this evening," he said.

"You're leaving Atlanta? But you just brought the boys here yesterday so that they could spend more time with you. This isn't on your itinerary. What's going on?"

"Leah, if you need any help with them you can call Doug. Just watch the boys for me, please. I'll explain everything when I get back."

Wayne hung up his phone and pulled out of the parking lot. He turned his car onto Peachtree Street,

then headed toward Interstate 85. Wayne realized that
it was time for him to do something he should have
done thirty-five years before. He was going back to Andrus, South Carolina, to claim his son.

Chapter Twenty

"Miss Minnie, you do not have to go to any fuss for us," Semaj said protesting. "I live alone in Atlanta, and I know how to cook."

"Hush up now," Miss Minnie answered. She swatted him lightly with her dishcloth. "I promised you that I'd take care of this property when you are not here, and I promised your grandma Nettie that I'd take care of you when she wasn't here. It's my pleasure."

Semaj and Rip had barely had time to get inside the house and put their suitcases down before Miss Minnie was knocking on the back door with a tray full of chicken salad sandwiches, homemade potato salad, almond drop cookies, and pink lemon tea. After the drive from Atlanta they both were very hungry and dug into the lunch she'd prepared for them.

As soon as they sat down at the kitchen table and began eating she told them she was on her way to the grocery store to pick up the items she needed to cook their dinner.

"I'm planning to make a chicken pot pie with a Ritz cracker crumb crust, pear salad, and for dessert, my blue ribbon–winning coconut brownies,"

The meal sounded delicious, and Semaj knew from experience that Miss Minnie was one of the best cooks in the state, but he didn't want to impose on her hospitality. He made a weak attempt to refuse, but she wasn't listening.

Rip tried his hand at dissuading her. "Miss Minnie, you know that I can cook. My aunt started teaching me when I was nine years old. How do you think I got so fat?" he laughed.

Miss Minnie laughed too. "Well, young'in, who do you think taught your aunt to cook? Now I've told you boys that I'm cooking tonight and every night that you are here." She paused for a moment. "You got any idea how long that's gonna be?"

"No, Miss Minnie, I really don't know. Things are kind of up in the air right now," Rip answered. He took a bite of his sandwich and chewed it slowly.

"What about your wedding?" Miss Minnie asked Semaj. "I've been looking forward to coming to Atlanta to see you jump the broom. Nettie would be so proud, God rest her soul."

Semaj looked at her strangely for several seconds without answering, and then Rip spoke up. "That's on hold too, for now. Miss Minnie, I know you are used to having the place to yourself. We promise not to be too much trouble," he said.

"He's right, Miss Minnie. Since you insist on cooking, we'll help out in other ways. Tomorrow, I'm gonna cut the grass and probably clean the gutters," Semaj said.

"Don't worry about doing yard work, man. I'll take care of that. Why don't you stay in the house and relax," Rip said.

Semaj put his sandwich down. "This is my house. You're a guest. How about *you* stay in the house and relax?"

Miss Minnie laughed at them, and they stared at her wondering what could possibly be so funny. "You boys have always been as tight as Dick's hatband. No matter what the situation, you have always stuck together and defended each other."

Before they could stop her, Miss Minnie began reminiscing about an incident from their childhood.

Rip and Semaj had been playing baseball in the field behind Minnie's father's house. At one time it had been a thriving garden, but as he got older he stopped planting things and grass and weeds overtook it. Because he no longer needed it, he allowed the neighborhood kids to use it as a playground. At the time he was getting on in years, and Minnie was living with him to take care of him.

"My daddy was lying in his bed watching his stories," Miss Minnie said. "He loved him some *As the World Turns* and *Another World*. When he was watching his stories he wanted everyone in the house to sit down and shut up. You boys was out in the back field hooping and laughing and playing baseball. Y'all remember that?"

They looked back and forth between each other, and then back at Miss Minnie. "No, ma'am, we don't remember," they both said.

"Well, I do. Anyway, I was just about to bring Daddy his lunch and just as I walked in the room, a baseball came crashing through the window. It bounced off the floor and smashed into Daddy's TV. The screen cracked, and everything went black."

Miss Minnie laughed hysterically and slapped her knee as she continued her trip down memory lane.

"I had never seen my daddy look so mad in my whole life. As sick as he was, I really thought he was gonna get out of that bed and beat the black off you two."

Rip began laughing along with her. He didn't remember the incident at all, but Miss Minnie told it with such enthusiasm that he was thoroughly enjoying it.

"So I walked out back and saw you two standing in the middle of the field arguing back and forth. I hollered for you to come inside and talk to Daddy 'cus he was mad as a wet hen. I watched y'all walking toward me still going back and forth arguing with each other and all I could do was shake my head 'cus I just knew y'all was arguing over what lie you was gonna tell. Well, I gots to say that when you got into that room, both me and Daddy were surprised by what we heard."

Semaj looked at her eagerly like a child hearing his favorite fairy tale. "What did we say, Miss Minnie?" he asked.

"Well, Rip spoke up first," she said.

"I'm sorry I broke your window, Mr. Shaw. It was all my fault. I don't have much money, but I'll find a way to pay for it somehow," Rip said.

"No, he didn't break it. I did," Semaj said interrupting him. "I broke your window and I'll pay for it."

Rip turned to face Semaj. "Don't lie for me, man. I broke the window. I pitched the ball, and that's why the window got broken. I'm gonna pay for it."

Staring him straight in the face, Semaj responded, "I hit the ball through the window, so it's all my fault, and I'm gonna be the one to pay for it."

"It's my ball. That makes it my fault," Rip said.

"It's my bat, so it's my fault," Semaj countered.

"Daddy had never seen anything like that in his whole eighty-one years of life, and neither had I. Instead of blaming each other, the both of you was trying to take the blame and protect the other one. Daddy was so impressed he had tears in his eyes. I gotta admit I got a little misty myself. He finally told y'all two to go on home 'cus he'd decided to fix the window and the TV himself."

Semaj leaned back in his chair and smiled. "I don't remember that, Miss Minnie, but you're probably right. We've always stuck by each other." He looked over at his cousin and smiled.

"Yes, you have, and no matter what happens, y'all need to always stick by each other's sides. Marion, you didn't have a father most of your life, and Semaj, your granddaddy passed when you was young. But you boys always have each other. Don't forget that."

Rip looked at her strangely. "Miss Minnie, are you trying to say that I was Semaj's dad and he was mine? We are the same age."

"That's not exactly what I'm saying, but in a way it's true. You made different choices in life, but God always brought you boys back to each other. That's no accident. Now I don't know all the details of what you two have done, and frankly, I'm too old to care. But I'm gonna say this, and then I'm going to Piggly Wiggly to get my groceries. Nettie used to have a saying that I still live by. Whatever is going on may not be a good thing, but you can best believe it's a God thing."

Miss Minnie kissed them both on the cheek, and then went out the back door.

"What do you think she meant by that?" Semaj asked.

Rip stood up and took his empty plate to the sink. He glanced out the back window that overlooked the driveway before answering "What did she mean by what?" he asked.

Semaj stared down at his plate, and he slowly shook his head. "What have we done, man?"

"Dang, this sink is clogged," Rip said suddenly. "You got a plunger?" he asked.

"Oh yeah, I'll get it from the utility closet."

As he walked down the hallway toward the other side of the house, Rip continued staring out of the window at a blue Cadillac Escalade pulling into the driveway.

It pulled up to the edge of the cement driveway and parked right under the basketball goal where Rip and Semaj used to play.

"I'll be right back," Rip yelled to Semaj.

Quickly he went out the back door and walked up to the door of the Escalade just as Wayne was attempting to get out. Forcibly he pushed it closed again, and with his arms outstretched, he leaned on the door preventing Wayne from opening the door.

Slowly the window rolled down. "Who are you?" Wayne asked.

"Who I am doesn't matter. I need you to leave. You shouldn't be here." Rip looked anxiously over his shoulder.

As he did, Wayne suddenly remembered seeing his photo on the news along with Semaj's the night the two were arrested. "Look, I know that you and Semaj were arrested, and that's why I'm here. I need to see him."

Rip shook his head. "No, you don't. I mean, now is not a good time. Trust me on this, Old School. Just stay in your car, back out of the driveway, and go home."

Wayne had a flashback as Rip called him Old School. "It was you. You're the one who brought me my food every day."

A look of panic washed over Rip's face. He looked over his shoulder again. "Just get out of here, man. I'm sure the police would not want the victim visiting with his alleged abductors. Just go, all right?"

"I just came from the police department, and I really don't care what they want. Now, move and let me out of the car." Wayne took a long deep breath. "I came to see my son."

From deep within, Rip reached down for a look that he had not used in a long time. It was the look he gave his drug runners if they dared to shortchange him.

It was the look he gave his rivals if they were stupid enough to step onto his turf. It was the look that meant "I am not playing with you, and if you value your life you will do as I say." It had put the fear of God into dozens of men, and Rip was now staring down Wayne James with it.

"This is your last warning, Old School. Back this piece of junk up and get out of here," he ordered.

The look worked its magic, and Wayne was terrified. He started up the engine and began backing out of the driveway. About halfway down he stopped. His conscience screamed loudly at him.

"The last time you were at this house to see your son you allowed an angry man to chase you away. He wouldn't even let you hold your infant son. Like a coward you walked away then, and now like a coward, you are walking away again. You should be ashamed of yourself."

Wayne quickly stopped the car and jumped out before Rip realized what he was doing. He faked to the left, then moved to his right and ran past Rip and bolted to the back door. He opened it and rushed inside with Rip closely on his heels. Semaj was standing at the sink with the plunger trying to figure out why Rip had believed it was clogged. The water was running freely for him. He heard the back door open, and he spoke without looking up.

"Rip, this sink is fine. Maybe you just needed to flip the switch for the disposal."

When Rip did not answer he stopped staring down the drain and looked up into the face of Wayne James.

"Hi, Semaj," Wayne said. He smiled broadly.

Semaj's face filled with shock and awe. "Wayne James? Oh my God, what are you doing here?" He reached out and enthusiastically shook Wayne's hand.

"I've been a fan of yours for as long as I can remember. I never dreamed that one day you'd be standing in my kitchen. Wow, this is definitely a pleasure."

Puzzled, Wayne looked at Rip for an explanation.

"I tried to tell you that it wasn't a good time," Rip said.

Semaj was beaming like a kid at the circus. He turned to Rip. "Cuz, you never told me that you knew Wayne James. Wow, this is mind-boggling."

For the first time since he'd entered the kitchen, Wayne noticed a small bandage above Semaj's right eyebrow. He also noticed that his cheek appeared to be bruised and his left arm was in a cast.

"What happened to you?" Wayne asked.

"I was driving along minding my own business and a big oak tree jumped out in front of me," Semaj laughed loudly. "So I took some time off work, and Rip brought me here to recuperate. As the saying goes, there's no place like home. This was my grandparents' house, but they are deceased now. I'm so sorry, excuse my manners. Would you like to have a seat?"

Still feeling confused, Wayne looked at Rip for help.

"Yeah, take a seat in the living room," Rip said. "Can I get you a diet soda?" He winked at Wayne to signal him to answer yes.

"That sounds good," Wayne answered. He looked back and forth at the two of them for a moment, then went into the living room and sat down.

"Semaj, I drank the last Diet Coke," Rip lied. "Can you run up to Miss Minnie's trailer and get one for . . . um . . . for my guest?"

Semaj happily agreed and went out the back door. Rip walked into the living room to explain everything to Wayne.

In the living room, Wayne sat quietly on the sofa and looked around the room amazed at how strong he could feel Allison's presence in the space. It was almost as if she was walking around in front of him or sitting beside him. There was an ashtray on the coffee table that she'd once told him she made when she was four years old. He remembered how she talked about her mother's hand knitted blankets, and he admired the intricate detail of the one draped over the back of the sofa. There was an old-fashioned upright piano sitting in the corner, and he imagined how Allison would have looked playing it. He looked on the wall at the family portrait hanging directly over the television. In the photograph was a very young Alvin and Nettie dressed in their finest Sunday clothes. Allison was seated in Alvin's lap wearing a lavender dress with white bows in her hair. Wayne imagined that she was no more than ten years old when the portrait was taken. Lovingly he stared at it.

"That's his mom," Rip said. He walked in and sat across from Wayne.

Wayne nodded his head. "I know. Allison was a beautiful woman, and I loved her very much."

"Why are you here?" Rip asked suspiciously. He was well aware that Wayne was Semaj's father, but the last he had heard, Wayne was denying that fact. He stared at him closely trying to figure out what he wanted.

"I told you outside. I came to see my son. I'm through denying him, and I just wanted to talk to him. He acts as if we've never met before. What's going on?"

Rip sighed heavily. "He doesn't remember meeting you. The fact is, he doesn't remember a lot of the last year. Some things are clear, and other things are fuzzy. He remembers his fiancée Ellen, but he doesn't remember proposing or making wedding plans. It's complicated."

"When did this car accident happen? It's only been a few days since you were released from jail," Wayne said.

Rip glanced toward the kitchen to make sure that Semaj had not returned. "He didn't have a car accident. That's just what he thinks, and I'm just not ready to tell him the complete truth yet."

"Then what happened to him? How did he break his arm?"

Instead of answering immediately, Rip went to the kitchen window to see if Semaj was returning. Miss Minnie had just gotten back from the store, and he was helping her carry in her groceries. With his one arm Rip imagined that it would take him awhile. He returned to Wayne in the living room.

"He was beat up in jail," Rip said as soon as he sat down.

Astonishment and anger covered Wayne's face. "Are you saying he was a victim of police brutality?"

"No, but the police are responsible for what happened to him. I've already contacted a lawyer to file suit. They are going to pay for this."

Wayne was getting impatient waiting to hear the rest. "Please just tell me the whole story," he begged.

"Well, after we were arrested and booked, the Atlanta police department had the stupid notion that they would not give Semaj any star treatment. The public was really angry with him as they felt they'd been tricked. People were protesting outside with signs calling him a fraud and a lot of worse things. So the police decided that they would show the public that they were on their side. Instead of putting him in solitary confinement, they released him into general population."

"That's crazy. They should have known better than that. He's a local celebrity. They should have known he would be harassed by other inmates."

Rip nodded his head. "I can handle myself. I spent most of my teenage years in juvenile detention. If they had not separated us, I could have protected him. Instead, they put him in a cell with Eric Sims. That dude is shelled."

"What does 'shelled' mean?" Wayne asked.

"Keep up with the times, Old School. It means crazy, out of his mind, shell-shocked." Rip took his index finger and made circles around his ear. "Anyway, he's a crazy person, and he hates Semaj. That was a lethal combination."

The more Rip talked, it seemed that Wayne felt more confused. "Because of the whole kidnapping thing he hated him?"

"No, that didn't have anything to do with it. Awhile ago Semaj rescued a little girl named Cyndi from a crack house where she was being held by Eric Sims. He'd snatched her from the playground in her neighborhood and was planning to do God knows what with her. I knew Semaj was looking for the girl, and I heard through some connections of mine where she was, and I told him."

They heard the back door opening, and Semaj rushed through the kitchen and into the living room dragging Miss Minnie by the arm. "See, I told you Wayne James was here," he said with pride.

Rip introduced everyone and managed to monopolize the conversation as best he could to keep Miss Minnie or Semaj from asking too many questions. After several minutes he convinced them to return to Miss Minnie's trailer to begin chopping vegetables for the chicken pot pie.

Just as they were about to leave, Miss Minnie asked Wayne if he'd like a slice of her famous Strawberry Supreme Cake.

"I put real strawberries in the batter and the icing. Then I top it off with fresh strawberries dipped in white chocolate," Miss Minnie said proudly.

"Oh, it sounds delicious, but I'm allergic to strawberries," Wayne said.

"I'm allergic to strawberries too," Semaj said. "What a coincidence."

As soon as Miss Minnie and Semaj were gone, Wayne turned back to Rip. "That cut on his head is so small. I don't understand how that could have caused him to lose his memory. None of this makes sense."

"The beating is not what caused him to forget you. That was just the last straw that finally broke the camel's back. You probably don't know it, but when you rejected him that day in the hotel room, my cousin flipped out."

Wayne shook his head. "No, he didn't. I mean, he was upset, but he didn't turn over any tables or act a fool."

"Well, you don't know him like I do. After that day, he turned into another person. It was a gradual progression that just got worse and worse. First, he disappeared without talking to anyone, and I had to drive here to find him. When he got back to Atlanta, he was lying to his fiancée. Semaj is the most honest man I know, but he was lying without a second thought. I admit it was my idea to kidnap you, but Semaj took it to a whole other level where he would just go into fits of anger out of nowhere. I was ready to let you go after one day, but he wouldn't let me. He went into a fit of rage because he was really out to get you. He wanted to publically embarrass you and make you pay for abandoning him as a child, and then rejecting him as an adult."

Wayne stared at the floor feeling ashamed for the way he'd treated Semaj. "I'm sorry. I didn't realize it had affected him in that way," he said quietly.

"Well, like I said, it was gradual at first and after you were freed I honestly thought that Semaj was finding his way back to his old self. He changed his mind about confronting you, and he and Ellen were back to making wedding plans. I thought things were all good, but I was wrong. He felt remorse, but he was still freaking out inside. Being arrested and beaten up in jail was more than he could take, I suppose. When I made bail, I found out that Semaj had been taken to Piedmont Hospital. Ellen and her family were with him when I got there. It was strange. He started talking, and the things he was saying just were not making complete sense. We still don't know why he thinks he had a car accident. We were worried, so me and Ellen went to talk to the doctor to find out what was going on with him."

Rip suddenly stopped talking, and Wayne looked up from the spot he'd been staring at on the floor. "Well, what did the doctor say?"

Sighing loudly, Rip continued. "In a nutshell, he says that because of the trauma and stress of this whole ordeal that Semaj has something called situational amnesia. The doctor assumed it was being arrested and the beating, but Ellen and I realized it started right after he was rejected by you. It began with the depression, then the lying, the agitation, the arrest, and finally, he just couldn't deal with it so he forgot it."

Wayne buried his face in hands. "It's my fault. That's what I came to tell him. Being abducted was the most frightening experience of my life. While I was being held I missed my other children terribly, and some days I wondered if I'd ever see them again. I also had a chance to think, and I realized that being locked in that warehouse was also the most eye-opening experience of my life. I never should have left my son years ago, and I never should have denied him."

Rip looked at Wayne James sitting in front of him filled with tears, grief, and remorse. He thought for a few moments; then he spoke.

"Look, I'm not a genie or a fairy godmother. Lord know I ain't no angel. But I think I just may have been given the ability to grant you one wish. There's just one catch. You have to wish for the right thing."

"The only thing I wish is that I could go back in time to the day Semaj found me and admit to being his father."

"Wish granted," Rip said. He smiled broadly feeling especially proud of himself.

Wiping his tears away, Wayne stared at him. "I don't understand."

"He doesn't remember that day, so you have the chance to do it all over again. I'll go get him from Miss Minnie's. All you have to do is tell him that you are his father. I don't know, but maybe that will help him get over the trauma he's experiencing."

Intrigued by the idea, Wayne suddenly began to perk up. "That won't solve everything. What about the kidnapping charges?"

"My lawyer has assured me that after the way they treated Semaj, the Atlanta police department will have a hard time moving forward with any charges, because they are going to be busy fighting the lawsuit we are gonna file on Semaj's behalf. In order to push it, they would need your cooperation, and I don't think you plan on helping them. Now do you?"

Wayne's face lit up with a mixture of anticipation and fear. "What am I going to say to him? What should I tell him?"

"Tell him everything you wished you'd said that day. Tell him about his mother, Allison. She's a mystery to him. It's real simple, Old School. Tell him the truth."

Rip stood up to leave, and Wayne grabbed his arm to stop him.

"I don't know if just starting over and pretending the last few months never happened is a good thing."

"I don't know if it's a good thing either. But I'm convinced that it's a God thing."

Without another word, Rip quickly went out the back door.

Epilogue

"Stop fidgeting," Jenise said to Ellen. "If you don't be still I will never get this thing laced up."

Ellen did her best to hold still. "I'm just so nervous. Semaj and I have been through so much the past six months. I was afraid we'd never get here. When I realized that he'd blocked out proposing to me, my heart was shattered."

Jenise continued looping the ribbons to her sister's dress and pulled them tightly. "You know that had nothing to do with how he feels about you. He was in a bad place because of his dad."

"I know that now, but it was touch and go for a minute or two."

The two of them turned around as they heard their mother enter the dressing room. She had a linen handkerchief in her hand, and it quickly went to dab her eyes.

"No tears, Mom, you promised. If you cry, we'll all cry, and then we'll all look like a raccoon family," Jenise said.

"I'm sorry, I can't help it," Deloris replied. "Both of you girls look so beautiful today."

Deloris was very proud that her firstborn daughter was getting married, but she also was elated to see Jenise looking healthy and happy. The six months prior had been difficult for her as well as she adjusted to life as a single mother without Reggie.

From his jail cell he'd written her love letters, expressive poetry, and he'd even sent her lyrics to a song he planned to dedicate to her. Jenise took everything he sent her and placed it inside her prayer box. The prayer box was an old box she'd found and taped up, then decorated it with purple paper she found at the dollar store. Whenever something arrived from Reggie she read it; then she placed it inside the box. One of the things she learned while attending the domestic abuse classes was to not be quick to react to the emotional blackmail. The ladies in her class taught that it was just another way to control her when an abuser was not around. Instead, she learned to seek God and pray for discernment. Everything went into the prayer box instead of being stored inside her damaged heart.

For his crimes, Reggie was sentenced to five years in prison. Several of her family members and friends had encouraged her to file for a divorce, but she had yet to make a decision. She'd written the words "divorce Reggie" on a piece of paper, and it too was still residing inside the prayer box.

In the meantime, she dedicated herself to taking care of herself, and most of all, Aaliyah. She continued to pray and know that when they were all healed in God's love, then a decision could be made.

Down the hall in the church pastor's office, Rip struggled to help Semaj get his bow tie on. "This is crazy. I can't tie one of these things," he said feeling exasperated. "Why didn't you just get a clip-on?"

"Ellen picked this out, man. You know that. All I was allowed to do was nod and agree with whatever she said."

Pastor Frederick sat behind his desk chuckling at both of them. He knew how to tie the bow tie, but he enjoyed watching his grooms sweat just a bit before stepping in. Finally when he saw Rip turn four different shades of red in frustration, he decided to step in and help.

"Do you have any advice for me, Rev?" Semaj asked as the reverend patiently and efficiently tied his tie.

"Keep God first and your wife second. Remember that you are the head of the house, but she's the neck. The head can't move without the neck."

Standing nearby, Rip began to laugh.

"Laugh if you want, but I've been married thirty-three years, and I live by the motto that a happy wife is a happy life."

They were interrupted by a knock at the door. Doug poked his head into the room. "Semaj, I just got a call from Leah. Wayne's plane was delayed. He's on his way, but he's running late. Your bell ringer, Leo is here, and so are the rest of your brothers. What you wanna do, man?"

Semaj was just about to answer when he remembered the Reverend's advice. "Go ask my bride-to-be. Tell her I agree with whatever decision she makes."

Semaj was still getting used to the fact that he had a father and five brothers. When he'd returned to his grandparents' house from Miss Minnie's that day and Wayne told him that he was his father, he almost fainted dead away on the floor.

Over the next few months, Wayne and Semaj slowly took their time getting to know each other and building a relationship as father and son. Wayne told Semaj everything that he could remember about Allison and their relationship together. He even admitted to him that he was wrong to walk away from him as a baby and not fight for his son in his life. Semaj asked him why he'd done it.

"It's simple. I was a coward. Your grandparents hated me for taking Allison away from them, and they were determined that I would not be able to take you away from them also. I could have fought them. I know that I should have fought them, but I was a scared kid that just walked away," Wayne had said.

Due to his memory loss, Semaj attended weekly therapy sessions to try to find the reasons he'd blocked things out and to bring his memories back. In the first few sessions, he had dribbles of memory. He recalled a story he'd reported on the news, a movie he'd seen at the theater, but nothing significant. He had frequent nightmares that resulted in his waking up screaming, but once awake, he could not remember what frightened him. Then one day during his therapy session it all came rushing back to him. He had spent the previous day with Wayne and his brothers at Six Flags over Georgia. It had been one of the best days of Semaj's life, but for some reason he wasn't happy. He felt upset and full of turmoil. It wasn't his usual appointment, but he needed to see his therapist to help him sort out his feelings.

As he sat talking about how wonderful it was to have Wayne James in his life, the memories he'd suppressed came flooding back like a tsunami. He remembered everything. Not one detail was missing, not even the beating he'd taken in jail. Semaj crumpled himself into a ball and cried like a tiny baby while his therapist quietly watched.

Semaj remembered that day he'd been beaten in jail very vividly. As he lay in the hospital bed, he suddenly found himself back in his car on his way to meet Gwen for the very first time. His head began to pound as he experienced the worst headache of his entire life. His temples throbbed, and he imagined blood vessels bursting inside his skull. Then, everything went black.

When he awoke again, he saw Ellen and her parents sitting around his bed. His arm was in a cast, and he was bruised. The last thing he remembered was being in the car, and he assumed he'd been in an accident. He didn't remember it at all, but at that point, he was afraid to tell them how confused and scared he really was. Instead, he took whatever Ellen or Rip told him at face value and agreed to attend therapy sessions in hopes of remembering what had really happened to him.

Although he finally had a clear memory of how Wayne James came back into his life, Semaj decided that it wasn't a memory that he wanted to share outside of this therapist's office. Instead, when asked, he recounted the story of meeting him for the first time at his grandparents' home in Andrus, South Carolina. Those closest to him knew the truth, and for Semaj, that was all that truly mattered.

The one memory he felt the most remorse at losing was the night he had proposed to Ellen. He realized how patient and understanding she'd been to quietly pretend that it never happened while waiting for him to regain his memory. He remembered giving her a diamond engagement ring, but he realized she was no longer wearing it.

So he decided to re-create the moment for her with Jenise's help. Semaj took Ellen back to the restaurant where he originally proposed. With Semaj's instructions, Jenise had convinced Ellen to wear the same dress she wore that night, and he wore the same shirt and tie. He'd also had Jenise sneak the ring out of Ellen's jewelry box so that he could present it to her again. After she said yes, he reminded her that she'd often said that it was the most wonderful night of her life, so he decided that rather than just telling her that he remembered it, he decided to allow her to live it all over again.

They'd had to change the date, reprint the invitations, and juggle the arrangements, but they were ready to become man and wife on their wedding day.

After speaking with Doug, Ellen decided that they would wait for Wayne to arrive. However, nearly an hour later, they were still waiting so they felt it would be not be fair to their guests to postpone things any longer.

At last they were standing at the altar ready to take their vows before God and their families to spend the rest of their lives together.

Semaj stood nervously with his bride on his left and Rip on his right. He glanced nervously over his shoulder. Standing in the back, behind the last pew, he noticed that Wayne had finally arrived. It wasn't his high school graduation, but his dad had arrived, just in the nick of time. Wayne stood there beaming with pride.

THE END

Readers' Group Questions

1. Do you have a family member that you are searching for?

2. Has the absence of a family member greatly impacted your life?

3. Jenise stayed in an abusive marriage because she felt God wanted her to. Do you believe that an abused woman should remain in her marriage because God hates divorce?

4. Do you feel that your local church has resources/help for women who find themselves in abusive relationships?

5. After Rip and Semaj kidnapped Wayne, did you feel they had gone too far?

6. Do you believe that a woman can adequately raise a son without a man in his life?

7. How do you feel that your local church is dealing with the problem of young men who do not have fathers in their lives?

8. Ellen decided to call off her wedding because she felt Semaj was acting like a different person. Have

you ever felt that someone you loved was changing? If so, how did you deal with that situation?

9. As Christians, we are expected to be strong and pray in the face of adversity, but Semaj did not. Have you ever been in a difficult situation and felt that before you turned to God you spiraled out of control?

Biography

Zaria Garrison is a Black Expressions Bestselling Christian fiction author. Her debut Christian novel, *Prodigal,* was nominated for Christian Fiction Book of the year 2010 by SORMAG (Shades of Romance). Zaria was also nominated for Christian Fiction Author of the year. She is the former co-owner and staff writer of *EKG Literary Magazine*, an online magazine geared toward all members of the literary community. Zaria can be reached online at zariagarrison@yahoo.com. She lives in Greer, S.C., with her husband and son.

UC HIS GLORY BOOK CLUB!

www.uchisglorybookclub.net

UC His Glory Book Club is the spirit-inspired brain-child of Joylynn Jossel, Author and Acquisitions Editor of Urban Christian, and Kendra Norman-Bellamy, Author for Urban Christian. This is an online book club that hosts authors of Urban Christian. We welcome as members all men and women who have a passion for reading Christian-based fiction.

UC His Glory Book Club pledges our commitment to provide support, positive feedback, encouragement, and a forum whereby members can openly discuss and review the literary works of Urban Christian authors.

There is no membership fee associated with UC His Glory Book Club; however, we do ask that you support the authors through purchasing, encouraging, providing book reviews, and of course, your prayers. We also ask that you respect our beliefs and follow the guidelines of the book club. We hope to receive your valuable input, opinions, and reviews that build up, rather than tear down our authors.

What We Believe:

—We believe that Jesus is the Christ, Son of the Living God.

—We believe the Bible is the true, living Word of God.

—We believe all Urban Christian authors should use their God-given writing abilities to honor God and share the message of the written word God has given to each of them uniquely.

—We believe in supporting Urban Christian authors in their literary endeavors by reading, purchasing and sharing their titles with our online community.

—We believe that in everything we do in our literary arena should be done in a manner that will lead to God being glorified and honored.

We look forward to the online fellowship with you. Please visit us often at *www.uchisglorybookclub.net*.

Many Blessing to You!

Shelia E. Lipsey,
President, UC His Glory Book Club